'The **Midnight Swan** is... perfect trilogy. Each book... and utterly spelling-binding... the prequel and Catherine Fisher enchants her reader from beginning ...

'Th... ...ch crossed with the magic of Narnia and the dark enchantment of a fairy tale and you get **The Midnight Swan**. This tale transports you seamlessly from rural Wales to magical lands.' Francis Hodgkin

'I enjoyed the previous two books in this series so I was expecting to enjoy this one. It exceeded my expectations! If you're looking for an easy to read, enchantingly magical adventure story, look no further than this book, indeed this series.' Roberta Reads

'This trilogy brings alive the magic of Welsh legends and Seren becomes a character of legendary value. I adored this trilogy and though I feel closure, I would welcome Seren back in future books!' Erin Hamilton

The Midnight Swan

Catherine Fisher is a poet and children's author from Newport in South Wales. Her books include the New York Times bestselling *Incarceron*, the *Snow Walker* trilogy and the Chronoptika series, and she was the first Wales Young People's Laureate.

The Clockwork Crow (Firefly 2018) won the Tir na N'og Welsh Children's Book Award, was shortlisted for the Blue Peter Book Award and the Independent Bookshop Week Book Award, and was nominated for the Carnegie Medal. Its sequel, *The Velvet Fox* was published in 2019.

The Midnight Swan is the third and final book in the trilogy.

The Midnight Swan

Catherine Fisher

Firefly

First published in 2020
by Firefly Press
25 Gabalfa Road, Llandaff North, Cardiff, CF14 2JJ
www.fireflypress.co.uk

A CIP catalogue record of this book is available
from the British Library.

ISBN 978-1-913102-37-1
ebook ISBN 978-1-913102-38-8

This book has been published with the support of
the Welsh Books Council.

Typeset by Elaine Sharples

Printed by CPI group UK

In Memoriam Molly Fisher

Contents

1

Seren Rhys is hot and bothered

Buy a sweetbread, buy a ribbon...
Buy a box that will not open.

'Look! Look at all the stalls! And there are boats on the river!'

Tomos was almost standing up in the pony cart in excitement; Mrs Villiers grabbed hold of him in alarm as the whole thing swayed. 'Do keep still, Master Tomos, please! You'll upset us all into the road!'

Denzil, who was driving, gave a snort of agreement and flicked the reins, so that the pony trotted faster. Heat rippled over the fields.

Tomos slid down. 'Please, Mamma, can we take a ride on a boat?'

Lady Mair was pinning the veil on her hat to keep the dust from her face. 'We'll be there very soon, dear, and then we'll see. Calm down now. Look at Seren. She's being very sensible.'

Seren, sitting on the warm leather seat, glanced up and blinked. She had been so deep in her own thoughts that she hadn't even realised they had arrived. Now she scrambled up next to Tomos and excitement swelled inside her.

'Oh, it looks lovely!'

The little town was decked out in all its finery for the Summer Fair. Gold and blue pennants rippled from windows and chimneys, and on the church flagpole a great red dragon flapped in the breeze. From the crowded streets rose all sorts of interesting smells and noises – Seren could hear hawkers crying their wares, the constant bleat of sheep, the lowing of calves and the loud, raw music of a hurdy-gurdy.

'I could have a toffee apple,' Tomos said, anxiously. 'Couldn't I?'

Lady Mair laughed. She seemed almost as excited as her son. 'Yes! And so will I.'

Mrs Villiers gave Seren a shrewd glance. 'You're not so chatty as usual, my girl. Feeling a bit sick? I have some ginger pastilles…'

'I'm fine, honestly,' Seren said hastily. 'Mmmm. Smell the honeysuckle!'

The hedges were high now on each side of the cart as Denzil eased it expertly down the steep, rutted lane. The wheels jolted; Mrs Villiers clutched the seat and held on.

'Lord! How dry and broken the road is!'

It was true. There had been no rain for weeks. The harvest would be a fine one, and the hedgerows were ablaze with flowers, but the water in the well at Plas-y-Fran was a long way down and Captain Jones had been worried about his thirsty cattle.

Tomos slid over beside Seren. 'What's wrong?' he said quietly.

'Nothing.'

'There is. You've been looking forward to this for weeks.'

'I am!'

'Not as much as you were yesterday.'

She frowned. But it was right he should know. 'Well, maybe. You see, it's the Crow.'

Tomos glanced round. He moved a little closer. 'He's not flown away or got himself broken, has he?'

'No. It's worse than that. Remember that letter that came yesterday? Addressed to me?'

Tomos nodded. 'Yes! You never get letters. You said it was from a girl you knew in the orphanage and…'

'That was a bit of a lie.' Seren went red. 'Well, a complete lie. Actually it was this.'

She pulled the letter out of her pocket and handed it to him, and then watched as he read it quickly, while Mrs Villiers was busy swatting flies.

The dirty envelope contained a scrap of paper that looked as if it had been torn from the bottom of a printed page. Scribbled on it was a hasty message.

Dear Miss Seren

I would be most grateful if you would pass on the enclosed letter to my brother. It is not good news. Please look after him. I cannot come at present in person, as I have certain, er, personal difficulties. I will be there as soon as they let me out.

I remain

Yours most sincerely
Enoch Marchmain

Tomos whistled. 'The Crow's brother? That tall, thin man?

Seren nodded.

'So what does it mean?'

Seren took the paper from him and tried to look like her favourite detective. 'Watson, you know my methods. First, you must examine the envelope.' She turned it over. 'Observe. The address is written with a pencil, and the writing is very scribbly. Notice the hurried S and the almost illegible Y...'

'Seren, stop being Sherlock Holmes and just...'

'So I deduce that it was written secretly, in a cramped place, with a small blunt pencil by a left-handed man who was very worried. Then there's the postmark. It might be London.'

'So...'

'And this.' She turned over the note and showed him the edge of the printing on the back. 'There's something faint here. I've gone over the letters in pen. I had to use a magnifying glass to make them out, but that's what they say.

The letters looked like a pale ink stamp with some so faint they had vanished away.

ARSHALS A PR S N

Tomos shrugged. 'It makes no sense.'

Seren tried not to look superior. 'If you had read Mr Dickens' novels it would.'

'I'm going to read them. One day.'

'Look. If I do this...' She took out a pencil and, as the cart rattled into the cobbled town, she wrote the letters M, E I and O.

'Oh!' Tomos stared. 'I see!'

Now the words were quite clear.

MARSHALSEA PRISON

'That's really clever, Seren. But prison! Does it means he's done some ghastly murder?'

Seren shook her head. 'No, silly. The Marshalsea is a place where you go if you can't pay your debts. Poor Mr Enoch must have run out of money. Maybe that's why he wrote to his brother.' She sat back, and then said, 'There was a sealed letter inside the envelope and I gave it to the Crow. He put on his little spectacles and read it.'

'What was in it?'

'I don't know.' She frowned. 'As soon as he'd read it he locked himself in the wardrobe and now he won't come out. All he says is "Go away, you stupid girl. Leave me alone in my misery and let me die in peace".'

'Oh dear,' Tomos said.

The cart rattled under the arch of the inn yard and stopped.

The pony whickered and blew. Denzil jumped down and stretched.

Lady Mair looked at Tomos and Seren. 'Now, this is my plan. We will meet back here at the inn for tea at four before we go home. The Captain will ride back with us. He's already here with Angus. Oh, I do hope Angus wins the big prize!'

Tomos grinned. Angus was the Plas-y-Fran champion bull. 'He should. He's enormous!'

'You never know,' Denzil muttered darkly, handing Mrs Villiers down. 'Lot of handsome cattle this year, I hear.'

Seren jumped onto the straw-scattered cobbles. Suddenly all she wanted was to forget her worry about the Crow's letter and explore the Fair. 'Can we go? Right now?'

'Wait.' Lady Mair took out her purse and gave them a sixpence each. 'Don't waste it all on nonsense.'

'Certainly not,' Mrs Villiers snapped.

'And if you want to see me judge the pigs, it will be at three.' Lady Mair sighed. 'It's such an honour and I want to do it well, but I am so nervous! What if I choose the wrong pig and offend some stout farmer!'

Tomos grabbed Seren's arm. 'You won't, Mamma. Anyway, Denzil will advise you.'

Seren turned to run with him, but Denzil caught her sleeve quickly. The small man put his lips to her ear. 'Be careful, girl. Keep the boy safe. Everyone comes to the Fair. Even *Them*.'

Seren looked at him, startled.

Then she nodded.

The Summer Fair was a joyous riot of colour and noise. The streets, normally so sleepy, were packed with people. Fairings and sweetmeats and pots and pans and ribbons and honey and jam were being sold at dozens of stalls. There were shooting games and big men smashing a hammer to make a bell ring, tug-o-war, foot races, and, in a tent by the church, poetry being made up and chanted in Welsh. The sound of it fascinated Seren; Tomos had to tug her away. There were competitions for the best flowers and fruit and puddings and pies. Dancing went on at the corners of alleys, and fiddlers played reels and jigs and sipped ale from foaming tankards. In the main square a wooden roundabout creaked, its horses rising and falling, steam gusting from its engine.

'Shall we go on that?' Seren said.

Tomos shook his head. 'No. It reminds me of the hateful Carousel and *Them*. Let's look in the mirrors instead.'

Seren frowned, thinking of Denzil's warning. *They* were the Tylwyth Teg, the Fair Family. Strange, silvery, immortal beings, They lived underground or in the hills. Twice now They had tried to steal Tomos away, and the Crow too. She looked round, determined. She would keep her eyes and ears firmly open. If They were here, she would spot Them.

'And don't worry about the silly old Crow!' Tomos ran towards the nearest tent. 'Buy him a fairing! That'll cheer him up.'

As she ran after him Seren thought that was a good idea, but the Crow couldn't eat anything and he would certainly never wear a ribbon. Well, maybe she could find something that would bring him out of his bad humour.

But the Fair was so wonderful she soon forgot everything else. She ate two liquorice dabs and a long unwinding stick of sherbet. She bit through the crunchy outside of a toffee apple into the white soft fruit. She threw balls at coconuts and small yellow wooden ducks. She ran screeching through the Hall of Mirrors seeing a whole row of stretched, gross, squat, shrivelled and enormously tall Serens.

She bought a red ribbon for Lily the maid, who had been disappointed not to come, and a gingerbread man for Gwyn the stable boy.

So by the time the church clock struck half past two she was hot and sticky and thirsty and red from the sun. Also, she had lost Tomos.

Suddenly worried, she looked around.

She was in the middle of the market square and a huge flock of ewes was coming through. She stood back between a stall selling copper kettles and some baskets of whelks and cockles that smelled really fishy, but the bleating ewes shoved against her and she stumbled back again, into a sudden space she hadn't known was there.

She turned.

Behind her was a small dark alley.

It was squeezed between two houses, and its

slanty strangeness made her take a few steps closer. Its walls were cobwebbed and its cobbles glittery. There was something not quite right about it, as if it led right out of the happy sunlit day. She was about to turn away, when she saw the nearest stall.

'Oh!' she said.

It was a little way down, against one wall. Its lop-sided trestles were piled with old junk, kettles and books, looking worn and tattered and wonderfully musty.

Seren hesitated, just for a moment. Then she hurried down into the dimness.

No one was there. A small lantern was propped on the top of a pile of china saucers, and a cup of ale, half-empty stood beside it.

'Hello?' she said softly.

Her voice rang round the stone walls and overhanging roofs. The Fair seemed very far away, its noises distant.

Next to the lantern was a sign. It read:

EVERYTHING ONE PENNY.

Seren was relieved, because that was all she had left.

The books were certainly old. They were piled

in dusty heaps, some of them spotted with mildew. They were bound in leather and calfskin, with their titles in worn gold letters. A few had metal clasps and locks and, when she prised them open and looked inside, they were written in languages she didn't recognise at all. One actually fell to pieces as she turned its pages; she glimpsed unicorns and manatees and impossible beasts but the pictures crumbled to dust even as she tried not to breathe on them. They were unreadable.

Disappointed, she pushed them aside and from the bottom of the pile, she pulled out something else.

It was a small casket, made of a dark metal.

Thousands of tiny stars glinted on its sides.

Beautifully painted on the lid, the face of a swan was staring out at her. Seren gasped. The Swan's gaze was so direct she almost thought it was alive, especially as the eyes were inlaid with some shiny silver foil.

It was a black swan, and it wore a diamond collar. All around the painting were some words. She had to turn the box to read them.

The Box of the Midnight Swan
If you can open My closed lid
Your heart's desire Inside is hid

Seren's eyes went wide. This might be just what the Crow was looking for! After all, his heart's desire was to be magicked back to human form. Could it really only cost one penny? It seemed too good to be true.

She tried to open it, but the lid wouldn't budge. She tugged and peered, to see if it was glued or stuck together, but no, there wasn't anything wrong with it, and no keyhole either. There must be some trick to it, or…

Something hissed.

Seren turned, quickly.

On the corner of the nearest house a gargoyle was carved. It was an ugly goblin face, with its tongue out, eyes wide-open, ears like bat-wings. Below it another peered round a pillar, goat-eyed and angry. Seren backed away.

There were more. A cheeky one between some ivy, a sly one under the eaves. She took another step, then took the penny out of her pocket. She held it up.

'I'm leaving this for the Box. I hope that's all right.'

Seren put the penny down on the stall. She hurried backwards with the Box under her arm; she had a horrible feeling that it would be a mistake to turn her back on the faces.

Then something tiny and cold as a needle touched her arm.

It was a raindrop.

But it hadn't rained for weeks!

Even as she thought it, a huge downpour began, roaring down on the dim alley, rattling in pipes and gutters, being spat out in fountains by all the gargoyle faces, turning the cobbles into a stream of water. Seren gasped; she turned and fled, and was it the thunder of the rain or were there padding feet on the cobbles hurrying angrily after her?

She was soaked. Her dress clung to her. Her hair was plastered across her eyes, and then small hands came out of the storm and snatched at her hair, grabbed her dress. She gave a shriek and pulled away and yelled, 'Leave me alone!' and burst out of the alley into blinding sunlight, and crashed straight into Tomos.

The Box fell on the cobbles.

Seren staggered back.

'There you are! I've been looking everywhere.' Tomos wore a jaunty neckerchief and his mouth was smeared with toffee. 'It's time to see Mamma do her judging. Come on!' He bent down and picked up the Box and looked at it curiously. 'What's this? Trust you to find some old stuff, Seren.'

'It's not for me. It's for the Crow.' She snatched it back from him. 'I got it from that stall down there…'

She turned. Her words dried up.

Between the copper kettle stall and the fishy whelks there was just a blank stone wall.

No alleyway.

No gargoyle faces.

No stall.

Not only that, it was sunny and she was completely dry.

Tomos wasn't listening. 'Tell me about it later.' He grabbed her arm. 'Come on, now, or we'll miss it all!'

Seren let him pull her away. But she kept tight hold of the Box, and took another look back, puzzled and scared, at where the alleyway should have been.

They had been angry. This was something secret, something They didn't want her to have.

But it was too late now.

2

Some worrying
questions

Iron horseshoes on the door.
Why ask what has gone before?

Next morning Seren sat up and tugged aside the curtain round her bed.

A shaft of bright sunlight was slanting across the darkness of the room, gilding the left paw of Sam the cat, where he lay sprawled out on the dressing table, watching her.

'Bore da, Sam,' Seren said sleepily.

It was a quarter to eight by the clock.

She looked down at her clothes on the floor. She had been so tired by the time they got back last night that she had done nothing but tug off her dress and scramble into bed.

Now she grinned, thinking of Lady Mair giving the prize for the best pig to a small bent man called Dai Hughes, who everyone had known would win because his sow, Anwen, was so white and fat. And their very own bull, Angus, had won best in show and been given a rosette to wear behind his ear!

She laughed out loud.

A sniff came from the depths of the room. A disapproving, tetchy sniff. 'Had a good time, did you?'

'Oh yes! It was such fun!'

'I'm so glad.' He didn't sound at all glad.

'Where are you?' she said quietly.

Sam jumped over onto her quilt and purred.

'No, not you,' she said, smoothing his head. 'You. Clockwork Crow.'

Silence. A rustle in the wardrobe.

'You're not still sulking in there?'

'I'm not sulking, silly girl,' he snapped. 'I'm cogitating.'

'Well, come and do it out here.'

Another creak, louder this time. A rattle. Then,

'I can't. The stupid door seems to have locked itself on me.'

Seren grinned. Pushing Sam aside she sat up, swung her feet out and went and tugged the curtains wide so that sunlight, already warm, flooded the room. She opened the casement and let in the soft, sweet, summer air. Then she unlocked the wardrobe and stood back.

The Clockwork Crow stalked out.

He was moth-eaten and his beak was bent and his black feathers were very ruffled, but he held his head high with rigid dignity. He flapped up to the windowsill, folded his wings and glared out at the sunny lawns and blue lake. 'Another glorious summer day! How lovely!'

Seren sighed. 'You're still in a bad mood.'

The Crow didn't even bother to answer.

She didn't like this. Usually he would have told her off for lounging in bed and then demanded answers to a whole list of nosy questions about the Fair: who was there, what they did, what they ate, who won what.

He would have been scornful and boastful and slyly interested.

She wished he would even tell her off. It would

be better than silence. She sat on the bed. 'So what was in your brother's letter?'

'None of your business.'

'Yes, it is.' Seren crossed her legs. 'Anyway I already know. Enoch is in London. He can't get here. Because he's in prison.'

The Crow almost choked. 'What!'

Seren tried to look modest. 'I deduced it. It was … elementary.'

The Crow was still spluttering. 'I can't believe…'

'I know it's a bit of a disgrace for your family. But if it's just for debt…'

'Stop. STOP!' The Crow held up a wing furiously. 'AT ONCE!'

She stopped.

The Crow drew itself up. 'How dare you sit there and tell me Enoch is in prison!'

'But … the envelope…'

With a flourish the Crow produced the letter. 'Read it for yourself, Miss Detective. I mean, I wouldn't want you to think I was telling lies!'

She took it and read it, and felt her face getting redder and redder.

It was headed 16 Marshalsea Lane, Preston.

'PR e S toN, not prison!' she whispered in dismay. Then she read,

Dear Brother,

I'm so sorry I can't get to you at present due to such a foolish mistake on my part. I stepped off a moving tram and I seem to have broken my big toe. (Left foot.) It's in plaster and I have to keep it still for a few days.

*Please don't feel upset. I was so sure that the alchemist in Wolverhampton would be the answer to your problem, and it was such a shame that he blew himself up just before I got to speak to him. But don't despair, dear brother! We will get you back to your human shape! Please don't do anything rash, and BEWARE of **Them** because as you know **They** can't be trusted in anything.*

Your affectionate brother,
Enoch.

'Oh.' Seren felt very small. 'Prison ... Preston ... it's an easy mistake to make.'

'Seren, I'm going to confiscate every detective story you have. They are total rubbish and quite clearly a very bad influence on your imagination.'

No! She couldn't have that!

'Poor Enoch,' she said quickly. 'His writing is just like him. Tall and thin and nervous. I hope his toe doesn't hurt too much.'

'Enoch needs to look where he's going. As for you,' the Crow folded its wings with grim intent, 'I intend double homework for a week and then…'

'I bought you a present,' she said quickly.

The Crow blinked. Its jewel-bright eye fixed on her. 'What did you say?'

'I bought you a present. From the Fair.'

'Oh dear. Some tatty ballad-sheet…'

'NO! A Box. A really interesting Box. Look. I'll show you.'

She went over to the drawer of her dressing table and opened it, remembering for a moment that last night, even though she had been so tired, she had not wanted to leave the Box out, as if it might be dangerous. She lifted it out now and put it on the table.

'It's this. It was on a sort of stall, but then the stall disappeared. I think it belonged to Them, because there were all these ugly eyes and faces, and I sort of stole it though I did leave a penny and They were angry and ran after me, and it rained but it couldn't have really because I wasn't a bit wet...'

The Crow was not listening. It was sitting very still and its eyes were wide as moons.

It was staring at the Box's starry cover.

'My goodness,' it said at last, in a faint whisper. 'My giddy goodness.'

Seren smiled happily.

'I knew you'd like it. There are words look, all around...' She reached out.

'NO!' The Crow snapped.

Seren's hand stopped in mid-air.

'Don't touch it! It could be a trap. It smells ... dark.'

From far below, the breakfast bell tinkled.

The Crow hopped closer, looked sidelong at the Box. Cautiously, it stuck out a talon to touch the dark lid, but drew back shaking its head. 'Breakfast first. Then lessons. I have to think about this.'

But as she dressed quickly and hurried out she looked back and saw that the Crow was sitting more upright, with the old greedy gleam back in its eye, and she smiled secretly to herself.

At breakfast everyone was busy telling tales of their day at the Fair. Lady Mair sipped her coffee. 'I did so enjoy it,' she said. 'And I think, dear, that it's given me an idea.'

'Really?' The Captain was reading his newspaper but he put it down politely. 'What about?'

'I think it would be wonderful to revive the Plas-y-Fran Midsummer Ball.'

'Oh.' Seren gasped through a mouthful of toast. She had a sudden vision of a room of swirling dancers and a band playing wonderful music. 'What, a dance? Here?'

Captain Jones laughed. 'We haven't had that since my father's day.'

'Exactly!' Lady Mair's eyes were shining. 'It's about time we started it up again.'

'You won't have much time. That's tomorrow night.'

'Will it be fancy dress?' Tomos's eyes lit up. 'I could be a pirate. With a cutlass!'

'I don't know about that, old man.' Captain Jones reached over and took his wife's hand. 'But if you really want to do it, my dear, go ahead. Have a chat with Mrs V, though. She'll have plenty to say, I'm sure.'

Lady Mair squeezed his fingers. 'Oh Arthur, it would be wonderful. I'll start at once.'

'And now I have some business to attend to.' Captain Jones stood and went to the door. Then he turned, a little reluctantly. 'I wonder, Seren, if you'd come to my study before your lessons. Just for ten minutes. Nothing important...'

Seren stared. 'Yes, of course.'

She glanced at Tomos, who made a puzzled face.

Had she done something wrong? For a moment, a thread of worry went through her.

As she ate the rest of her toast and licked the orange marmalade from her fingers she tried to think what it was. Nothing really bad came to mind, though they had broken a little window in the stables with the cricket ball, but Tomos had hit it; she had just been bowling.

It couldn't be that.

When breakfast was finished, she waited till Tomos had run upstairs and Lady Mair had gone out to her sitting room, and still she sat there, at the crumb-covered table, thinking.

Maybe they were going to send her away to school.

It had to happen sooner or later. There were no schools near Plas-y-Fran. Tomos would go to boarding school next year – he said he was looking forward to it, but she wondered if that was true. Sometimes he seemed a little nervous about the other boys, and the masters, and all the hearty games and sports. She knew all about living with other girls, and she didn't really want to do that again.

And it wasn't as if they didn't have an expert teacher of their own!

She grinned, rubbing the crumbs with the tip of her finger.

Lily the maid came in. 'Finished, miss?'

'Oh yes, diolch, Lily.' She stood and went out and along the corridor.

The Crow was their teacher. Of course it was all top secret. Lady Mair thought that Tomos and Seren went to the schoolroom and taught themselves from books. When she tested them on Latin and Greek and History and Geography she was always startled at how well they were doing. 'Quite extraordinary!' she had said last time. 'I don't know how you children are so clever!' And the Clockwork Crow, who had been perched listening behind the waxed fruit dome, had smirked and preened himself with pride.

But that couldn't last either.

The Crow had to find his human shape again, and they had to help him.

It was only fair.

The house was lovely on a summer morning like this. All down the corridors dust hung in the slants of sunlight from the high windows. Doves cooed from their perches on the eaves, and the casement hung open so that Seren could hear the hum of bees in the lavender on the terrace below, and smell the sweet honeysuckle that climbed the garden wall.

She was so lucky to live here!

As she ran along the upstairs corridor her fingers brushed the panelwork. The house was safe now. There had not been a whisper of the Tylwyth Teg since Mrs Honeybourne's strange scarlet coach had disappeared into a flurry of leaves last autumn.

Denzil had iron horseshoes hanging over every doorway, and when Captain Jones had laughed at him about it he had just shook his head and said darkly, 'Better safe than sorry, Captain. Better safe than sorry.'

So there was no need to worry. But, as she came to the door of the Captain's study and stood outside looking at the brass doorknob, there was one tiny fear inside her that she didn't even want to name.

She knocked, lightly.

'Come in.'

She peeped round the door. 'It's just me.'

'Oh come in, Seren, please. It won't take a minute.'

She came in and stood in front of the desk. It was a big wooden structure, with estate documents littered across it, and letters and a pipe-rack. The whole room smelt sweetly of tobacco; it must be, she thought, just how Mr Sherlock Holmes' rooms in 221b Baker Street must smell.

'Well now. Sit down.'

She looked round and saw that a stool had been pulled up; she sat on it.

Captain Jones was a tall man. He walked up and down looking out of the open windows. He seemed a little bit nervous, she thought. 'Well,

Seren. I've been wanting to talk to you for a few days now. It's … ah … a little bit… Um … well, it's something I've been thinking of for a while.'

'About me?'

'In a way. Tell me, Seren,' he turned quickly. 'You are happy with us here, aren't you? At Plas-y-Fran?'

She stared at him, wide-eyed. 'Of course I am,' she said. 'I love it here, with Tomos and Gwyn and you and Lady Mair and the Cr … cats and doves and everyone. Denzil and Mrs Villiers and Lily. I love everything about it.'

She felt a bit frightened. How could she explain that Plas-y-Fran was the best place she had ever been in all her life and that she never, never wanted to leave? She couldn't, so she just said, 'It's home.'

'That's quite right. It is.' But he didn't seem quite satisfied, she thought.

He rummaged in the papers on the desk. 'All I want, Seren, and I'm sorry if this is a bit strange, is a few details from you about your life before you came here.'

She was really worried now. 'Before…?'

'Yes. I mean, your father was a great friend of

mine when we were both boys. We went to school together. I was at his wedding to your mother and then he asked me to be your godfather at your baptism. I held you at the font. Goodness, you were so tiny then! But when he went away to India I didn't hear much from him. I had a letter saying he was doing well and that was about all.'

She nodded. Why was he telling her this?

'I do blame myself that we lost touch. I went into the army, and met Lady Mair and got married and I had no idea that my dear old friend Roger had died, and his wife too, and that his daughter was in an orphanage. I do wish I had known earlier, Seren.'

'That's all right,' she said kindly, because she didn't know what else to say.

'So what I want you to tell me is … do you have any other relatives? Aunts? Cousins? Anyone at all?'

Seren frowned. 'My aunt died. I don't know about anyone else.'

'No one has ever written to you saying they were your family?'

'No.'

'I see. I thought not, but… Of course your

aunt's solicitor might be able to help. I have already written to him to enquire.'

Seren fidgeted on her chair. Written to the solicitor! That sounded bad.

Captain Jones sat at his table and dipped a pen in the inkwell. He made notes of her full name, Seren Elinor Rhys, her date of birth and anything she could remember about her family, which wasn't much, because before the orphanage everything was a blur. She was tempted to make a few things up, but something stopped her. Captain Jones wrote it all down, and then blotted the page dry. 'Well. That will have to do. You'd better run off to your lessons now. I'm sorry to have kept you from your fun.'

But Seren didn't move. She clasped her hands together on her lap and asked the question that was tormenting her. 'Are you going to send me away? To school? Is that it?'

Captain Jones looked surprised. 'School? Is that what you would like? I hadn't thought… Oh, goodness! Look at the time!'

The grandfather clock in the corner was chiming ten softly. 'I'm sorry, Seren.' Captain Jones swept the papers into the drawer and locked it, and hurried to the door. 'I have a meeting at the bank and I have to run or I'll be late. Have a good morning, my dear.'

He ushered her briskly out and strode off.

She was alone in the corridor.

3

A small brown photograph

Shake and rattle, test and weigh
You can't measure the heart's dismay.

Seren gazed after him. Then she began to walk slowly towards the schoolroom.

What was going on? Those forms and papers worried her. They reminded her of interviews with inspectors at the orphanage, who were always big men in dark suits and top hats, who wrote things down gravely and shook their heads a lot.

A sharp whistle made her look up.

Tomos was peering round the schoolroom

door. 'Where have you been? He says, fetch that Box. But be careful and wear gloves.'

Seren sighed. Sometimes the Crow was just silly. She ran to her bedroom, put on her church gloves and picked up the Box carefully, wrapping a shawl around it just in case. Then she hurried to the schoolroom.

'Put it down there.' The Crow flicked a wing at the cleared table.

Seren did. She stepped back. 'What shall we…?'

'Lessons first,' the Crow snapped. 'Box later.'

She frowned at Tomos. They both knew the Crow was itching with excitement to examine the Box, but this was just like him, to pretend it was an ordinary day with nothing unusual going on.

For five whole minutes they tried to do Latin translation. But Tomos got the tenses all wrong and Seren forgot the words and even while the Crow tutted and strutted, its bright eye kept straying to where the dark Box lay shimmering in the sunlight on the table.

Finally Seren threw down her pen. 'This is just totally silly! No one can concentrate. Let's get on with it!'

The Crow managed half a second of looking

cross. Then it flipped the chalk it was trying to write with across the room. '*Kek kek*,' it said. 'You're quite right. Come on.'

It flipped across to the table. Tomos slapped his notebook shut and hurried over. They gathered round the Box.

Seren put out her hand but the Crow slapped it back. 'NO! This could be dangerous. We have to conduct a thoroughly scientific investigation.'

Tomos grinned but the Crow was deadly serious. It hopped all around the Box, tipping its head and eyeing every inch of the sides.

Then it jumped back.

'Scales,' it demanded.

Seren carried the heavy weighing scales over to the table.

'Put it on.'

She put the Box in one pan and some weights in the other, until the pans were level, and Tomos read the weight on the scale. 'Twelve ounces.'

'Heavy. Write that down.'

Seren grabbed a pencil and scribbled it on an empty page. Then she wrote THE BOX OF THE MIDNIGHT SWAN on the top, just for a heading.

'Measuring tape!'

Tomos ran for it. The Crow took one end in its beak and stretched it out, but got it all tangled round his talons. 'Drat!'

'Let me.' Tomos measured the Box carefully. 'Nine inches by seven inches. And three inches deep.'

Seren wrote that down too. 'Why are we doing all this?'

'Always study the artefacts of the enemy.' The Crow sniffed the Box and then touched it with the very edge of a feather.

'It's not going to explode.'

'You never know with Them,' the Crow said darkly. 'Thermometer!'

It took a while to find one; Seren had to run down to Gwyn in the hot-house and borrow one off the wall, and then hurry back with it.

'It's probably just the same temperature as the room,' Tomos said as they watched the red line of mercury fall and steady.

'It's a lot colder. And that,' the Crow put on his best lecturing voice, 'would suggest a supernatural, even sinister, component within that might…'

Seren frowned. She was fed up of waiting. 'But I want you to read the words!' She reached over the

Crow's shoulder. Then she gave a great cry of surprise. 'It's gone! How is that possible?'

She was amazed. There was no beautiful black swan gazing out at her from the lid. Instead the picture showed a dark lakeside, the deep water seeming to ripple on the shore, the trees shadows with stars caught in their topmost branches. Beyond, barely visible, were the turrets of an enormous castle with one lighted window in the highest tower.

In the grass sat a hare and a tiny mouse. High in a tree perched a white owl.

'It's a completely different picture!'

'Hmmm.' The Crow pushed imaginary glasses up its beak. 'I didn't see anything else.'

'Neither did I,' said Tomos. 'It's always looked like that.'

'No, it hasn't!'

'What was there before?'

'A black swan. Wearing a collar.'

The Crow blinked. It stared at her, astonished. 'A collar? *A diamond collar*?'

'Yes. And the words…'

Tomos said, 'There are no words.'

Seren took a breath. She picked up the Box and

stared. 'Yes, there are. I don't know why you can't see them. Perhaps it's magic. I'll read out what it says.'

The Crow nodded, doubtful. 'As long as you're not making this up...'

'I'm not!' So she read the words out loud.

The Box of the Midnight Swan
If you can open My closed lid
Your heart's desire Inside is hid

'Now can you see why I bought it for you?'

The Crow didn't answer. Its beak was hanging open and its eyes were wide with sudden dismay.

'No!' it whispered. 'No. It can't be...'

'What?' Seren said.

The Crow couldn't take its eyes off the Box. It began talking very fast. 'Right. Yes. Very well. I think we should just stop this now and go back to Latin. Maths, even. *Playtime!* Yes, let's have playtime. We can get out the jigsaw puzzles and the chessboard. Table skittles...'

'What on earth are you gabbling about?' Seren said. She had never seen the Crow in such a panic. 'It's not dangerous. I can't even get it to open... See...'

She showed them how the lid refused to move. Tomos tried too. He was baffled. 'It's as if it's locked,' he muttered, irritated. He picked the Box up and turned it over. 'Something's stuck on the bottom.'

Seren stared. 'There wasn't before…'

'Well, it's a magic Box, that's for sure. Look.'

He peeled something small and brown off and it slipped from his fingers and fluttered to the floor.

Before Seren could move, the Crow had hopped down, he grabbed it in his beak and was staring at it.

'*Kek kek,*' he gasped.

'What is it?'

The Crow didn't answer for a moment. Then he said, in a rather strangled voice, 'Nothing. Just an old photograph.'

'Let me see.'

'No. I…'

But Seren had already snatched it. She and Tomos looked at it eagerly.

It was very old, all sepia-brown and faded. It showed a man. He was thin and hook-nosed and dressed in old-fashioned dark clothes and he was standing in a garden. It looked like a rose garden because there was a rose in his fingers. A white rose with a long straight stem.

'Totally uninteresting,' the Crow gasped, turning his back on it. 'Right, let's have an early lunch.'

'What's the matter with you?' Seren folded her arms. 'Do you recognise him?'

'Of course not! Never seen him before in my life.'

Tomos looked at her and raised an eyebrow.

She nodded. 'We think you do! What's going on? Tell us!'

The Crow preened and huffed and *kek kekk*ed for a full minute. 'Don't order me about, child. This Box is clearly a trap set for us and...'

'Maybe it is. But it's more than that. You know about this Midnight Swan, don't you?'

The Crow looked down and tapped a talon.

'He does, you know,' Tomos said.

'I might.'

'So tell us.'

'I can't. It's ... not for children.'

Seren snorted. 'Tell us. Or next time your clockwork runs down I won't even bother winding you up.'

The Crow looked so unhappy she felt a bit of a bully. So she said, 'Please! We'd really love to help.'

But at that moment the lunch gong rang from below. The Crow looked heartily relieved. 'Ah. Now. You have to go. Wrap that Box up, Seren, in that shawl. And lock the door.'

She didn't move. 'You have to trust us. We can't help you otherwise. It can't be that terrible, can it? It might help us think how to get this Box open and find your heart's desires. To get you back to your human shape so that you can wear slippers and eat toasted cheese again.'

The Crow sighed. 'You are a most obstinate and annoying little girl. But, well … you are right. I have … er … come across the Midnight Swan before. It's not a very flattering story but I suppose I will have to tell you. Meet me after luncheon down at the summerhouse by the lake.'

'Promise?'

'I promise.'

'You won't lock yourself in the wardrobe?'

'No. Now go, before Denzil comes looking for you.'

Lunch was a chatty meal; Tomos and Lady Mair were still full of the Fair and the things they had seen and done. Seren ate her cawl and then was glad to see the cool dish of lemon syllabub, her favourite thing ever. She ate it, savouring every spoonful.

Lady Mair laughed. 'You're enjoying that.'

'We never had puddings in the orphanage.' Seren said it absently, and was surprised to find the remark produced an awkward silence.

'Oh dear,' Lady Mair said. 'That is so sad.'

Seren glanced at Tomos, He had looked down at his dish when she mentioned the orphanage. What was going on? And did Tomos know about it?

'Well, I've started on the invitations to the ball.' Lady Mair smoothed out a corner of the tablecloth. 'It's going to be the most splendid thing we've had here for years. I'm going to need your help later, you know, planning the children's games and the high tea.'

Tomos nodded.

'Will we get to hear the music?' Seren said wistfully. 'And watch the dancing?'

'I don't see why not.' Lady Mair stood up. 'Have a good afternoon. Are you going out?'

'To the lake,' Tomos said.

A small frown furrowed his mother's eyes. 'Oh. Do be careful. Perhaps Denzil…'

'We'll be fine.' Tomos grinned. 'Honestly.'

When his mother was gone, he jumped up. 'Come on, Seren! Finish that and let's go. I'm dying to hear what story the Crow is going to make up this time.'

Seren licked the last morsel and rattled the spoon in the dish. 'Tomos,' she said. 'They're not going to send me away, are they?'

He stared at her, amazed. 'Of course not! What ever made you think that? This is your home now.'

'But there's something going on.'

Tomos laughed and ran for the door. 'You and your imagination! I'm going to get my sun hat. See you there.'

He ran out leaving the door open, and Lily came in and began clearing the dishes. 'Have you finished with that, bach?'

'Oh yes. Diolch, Lily.'

Still, she sat for a moment wondering. Tomos had laughed. But it hadn't been like his usual laugh.

Not at all.

Denzil was in the hall, mopping the tiles. She walked carefully round the wet bits.

'You'll have a lot of work with this Ball,' she said.

Denzil stopped. He looked up at her and she was surprised at how dark and grave his face was.

'That's not what worries me.'

'What?'

'Use your head, bach. Who is it that loves dancing and music? Who is that wants only to enter the Plas and fill it with Their magic?'

Seren stared. She took a step closer. 'The Tylwyth Teg? But…'

'The Plas all lit up and music everywhere?' Denzil frowned. 'Oh, They'll be crowding outside, girl. You wait and see. They'll be so hungry to get in. That's dangerous.'

'Don't worry, Denzil. You've got your iron horseshoes up and yarrow and all sorts of protection. They can't get past that.'

'No.' He swished the mop in the bucket. 'Not unless They are invited. And who would be doing that?'

Seren nodded. She ran out into the brilliant sunshine. The afternoon was already hot, a scorch of butterflies. She turned a cartwheel, but it was too hot for that, so she wandered lazily over the green grass to the door in the garden wall, and through the flower beds of the sunken garden, brushing the tips of the blooms with her fingers so that the perfume of lavender and phlox and honeysuckle mingled with the drowsy buzz of bees.

The iron gate out onto the park was hung with a row of dangling iron things, shears and old knives and a horseshoe, hot to the touch.

Denzil was certainly taking no chances.

She stopped and looked back.

On the highest eaves of the house a small gathering of starlings sat in a row. Their eyes were bright and they didn't peck and shuffle but sat silently and intent.

They were watching her.

Even when she waved at them, they didn't fly away.

4

A difficult
story is told

Wings and feathers and cogs and wheels.
I wish you knew how strange it feels.

The summerhouse was a small thatched building
by the lakeside, all lopsided and frail. It always
looked as if it would collapse in the next high
wind, but it never did.

Seren ducked her head under the doorway and
saw that Tomos was already there, and that he was
on his hands and knees pulling out yellow
cushions from the locker under the wooden
bench, and the croquet balls and mallets as well.

'We could play a game later if you like…' Lying

flat, he dragged hoops from the back of the cobwebby darkness.

'I don't mind.' Seren sat on a cushion and stretched her legs out. 'Is the Crow here?'

'Not yet.'

She listened to the birdsong. It was sweet and distant, from the woods. On the lake, coots and mallards were diving for deep weed and insects. The surface of the water was a shimmer of yellow iris and pondweed and the flat plates of water lilies, skimmed by dragonflies with shiny wings.

She fanned herself with her hat. It was lovely to sit in the shade.

'I'd like to live here for ever and ever.'

'Yes,' Tomos said absently. He dragged out the last croquet hoop. Something else came with it. 'Oh,' he said. 'Look at this.'

She leaned over. It was a very small fountain pen, all marbled green. Its nib gleamed like gold.

'How did that get there?'

Tomos shrugged. 'It's probably my mother's. She often brings her sewing and writing stuff out here. Maybe she dropped it and it rolled under there. I'll ask her. It's really nice, anyway.'

Seren opened her mouth to answer but there

was a flutter of wings and the Crow swooped in and landed rather awkwardly on the wicker rail.

He looked around. '*Kek kek*. This place is hardly secure. But at least we're away from the house.'

'No one's listening, if that's what you mean.' Tomos put the pen in his pocket.

'Don't you be so sure,' the Crow said darkly. 'Anyway, I've put a silencing spell over it now. Just in case.'

'Is that why the birds have stopped singing?' Seren asked, noticing.

The Crow sniffed. 'Actually no. They're all too busy laughing at me. I had a few small … accidents on the way here. Someone moved a wheelbarrow in my way, and that oak tree certainly wasn't there yesterday.'

'Is that why your tail feathers are all stuck out?'

The Crow preened hastily. Then it hopped a little closer on its bent-wire talons.

Seren pulled her knees up and hugged them. Tomos sat cross-legged on a cushion.

They waited.

'Right,' the Crow said. 'So. Yes. I'd better start, then.'

It hopped a few times, restlessly. Then it took a breath, and cocked its head on one side. 'Just remind me. Have I ever actually told you the unfortunate story of how I came to be trapped in this horrible body of a Crow…?'

'Several times,' Seren said sternly. 'And every time it was different.'

'Ah…'

'First you told us you were a prince and that a witch magicked you into it because you wouldn't give her your jewels and your horse and your crown…'

'Hmmm. That's not a bad story…'

'And unless you gave up the one thing that meant most to you, you would never get back to human shape.'

The Crow sighed. 'It's not exactly true.'

'No.' Seren settled herself more comfortably. 'We know that. The second time you said you were a professor who wanted to learn to fly so you read out a spell from an old book, and it went horribly wrong.'

The Crow squirmed. 'Did I? I don't remember that one…'

Seren waved a bee away from her nose. 'I'm not

49

surprised. So maybe it would be best if you just told us the truth.'

'The truth?'

'What really happened.'

The Crow looked nervous. It hopped from foot to foot. Then it scratched itself so hard dust flew out. 'Goodness. I ... er ... well!'

'You see,' Tomos said, balancing a croquet mallet between his fingers, 'we think you did something bad and you're ashamed and you don't want to tell us about it. But we won't laugh or anything, honestly.'

The Crow stared at him with its jewel-bright eyes. 'What a relief!' it said acidly. 'Two foolish children who know absolutely nothing about anything won't laugh at me! I'm so happy! I'm so DELIGHTED! I could...'

'Stop wasting time,' Seren said kindly. 'You'll feel much better when you've owned up, you know. That's what people always tell me, and it's true. Well, a bit.'

The Crow was still for so long she wondered if its clockwork had run down.

'Do you need winding up...?'

'*No.*' The Crow lifted its head. Suddenly it began to speak quickly, as if to get it over with.

'I wasn't a prince or a professor. I was a schoolteacher. I lived in a small village in a valley not far from here. It was about … two hundred years ago.'

'TWO HUNDRED!' Tomos stared.

'About. And that's one of the problems about the unspelling … I have to be careful I don't just turn into a pile of dust … anyway, stop interrupting. Let me get on.'

'I didn't…'

The Crow silenced him with a glare. 'So, I admit I was not the most handsome of men. A little lean, a little hook-nosed. But I had a sort of … dark dignity. I was respected. People looked up to me.' It preened a feather, smoothing the barbs very carefully.

'I'm sure you were,' Seren said. She was fascinated. This had to be the true story, at last.

'My name was Mordecai Marchmain.'

Tomos choked on a chuckle. Seren pressed both her lips together tight so she wouldn't even smile.

'That's an unusual name,' she said.

'It's a very old and distinguished family.' The Crow drew itself up with pride. 'We are certainly

51

descended directly – in the maternal line – from Prince Llywelyn ap Gruffudd himself. So I may be, if you think about it, actually, a Prince of Wales.'

Seren nodded. It was important not to interrupt him now.

'So … I … er … I was very fond of a young lady. She was the daughter of the local squire, and extremely pretty, though perhaps not the most clever of girls. Anyway, one day I was on my way to Llangollen for the day and I was unwise enough to ask her what she would like me to bring her back for a present. I expected her to say a brooch, or some trinket. But she asked for a white rose.'

'Well, that's not difficult.'

'It is if it's the middle of winter! There was snow on the ground, for goodness sake!' The Crow shook its head. 'I asked her to choose something else but she wouldn't. She kept on that it was a test of my devotion and if I truly loved her I would get it and all that sort of nonsense. Now, of course, I would think her extremely foolish but then I was young and, er, rather in love.'

Tomos grinned at Seren. She frowned back.

'Well, it was a difficult journey to Llangollen through the snow, and after I had completed my business, I tried the shops and markets there but, of course, there was no such thing as a white rose to be had for any amount of money. I bought her a box of truffles and set off back home. By this time, it was very late, almost midnight and snowing heavily. I had snow in my eyes and hair and on my face, and it was impossible even to see the way. After about an hour or so I found myself on a track deep in a gloomy wood. I came to a crossroads where four lanes met. There was no signpost, so I guessed and took what I thought was the right path. That was a mistake! Soon I was completely lost. I was trudging down tiny winding ways that seemed to lead nowhere but around on themselves as if I was walking in ever smaller circles. The snow was getting deeper. I was quite worn out, and rather afraid I would just die in that wood. And then, suddenly, there was a high stone wall, with a door in it.'

'What did you do?' Tomos asked.

The Crow fixed him with a glare. 'What do you think, silly boy? I made my way to the door. It was banked with snow and brambles, as if no one ever opened it, which was not at all comforting. There was a bell-pull; I pulled it, but heard no jangle, and no one came. I was shivering and there was snow on my shoulders. I had no choice. So I…'

'…opened the door!' Tomos gasped. He was sitting up now, tense with excitement.

'Am I telling this story or are you?' the Crow snapped.

'Sorry. You are.'

'So keep quiet. Yes. I opened the door. I went in. And that's when the strange things started to happen.' It paused.

'Oh, go on!' Seren groaned.

The Crow shrugged. 'I walked into summer.'

'Summer?'

'A summer garden. I stepped right out of winter into a glorious warm starry night. The garden smelled so sweet, and it was full of flowers. The trees were heavy with leaves and pollen, oak and ash and thorn. Bees and insects flitted between the branches. And a silver moon hung over a dark lake.'

'Amazing!' Seren muttered. She was really enjoying the story.

'Indeed. So much so I found it rather hard to believe. Was I dreaming? I looked round and even called out but there was no sign of anyone. Outside the gate was the snowy wood. I turned back and, over the treetops, I could just make out the grey turrets of a castle. Now, in this garden there were some beautiful roses...'

'I know! I know what's going to happen!' Tomos scrambled excitedly up onto his knees. 'You...'

The Crow folded its wings. He looked mortally offended. 'That's it. I'm not going on.'

'Please!' Seren begged. 'Please do!'

The Crow took a deliberate minute. It preened its ruffled feathers. Tomos fidgeted; Seren glared him to stillness. He had to let the Crow tell the tale. Or they'd never hear the truth.

Finally the Crow smoothed a last barb and said, 'Well. The roses. I suppose it was wrong. I mean they didn't belong to me. I would have left money, you know. I just wasn't given the chance. Anyway, as you guessed, I did a most foolish thing. I took out my knife and cut a white rose, with a long stem and dewdrops on its petals.'

'I knew it,' Tomos whispered.

The Crow ignored him. 'Immediately the gate in the wall behind me clanged shut. Thunder rumbled. Lightning flashed. All the flowers in the garden turned their heads to look at me. And the white rose in my hand began to sing.'

'*Sing*?'

The Crow nodded. 'That's the only word for it. Not like a human singing. A pure, high, silvery song. A terrible lament. Like nothing I'd ever heard. I wanted to drop the rose immediately, of course, to throw it away. I actually tried. *But my fingers were stuck to its stem.*'

'Gosh!' Seren shivered. Suddenly the summerhouse seemed cool, as if touched with a sinister, silvery magic. She edged into the warm sunlight.

'I couldn't get rid of it. I shook it, then pulled at it with my other hand, but that was worse because now both my hands were stuck to it! And still it sang that terrible song.'

'Were you scared?'

'No. Not… Well…' the Crow shrugged. 'Maybe just a little. And then the owner of the garden came.'

Tomos lay on his stomach. Seren sat very still. They both knew something tremendous was going to happen next.

The Crow was still a moment, as if remembering. Then he said, 'The lake was dark and the stars were glinting on the water. Ripples started to lap against the shore. I felt as if all the magic of the garden was being somehow gathered together; my skin tingled, my scalp shivered. And then, in complete silence, I realised that seven swans were swimming towards me out of the dark. Six of them were pure white, but the seventh, the one at the back, was deepest black. Its neck was long and graceful. Its eyes were glimmers of anger. And around its neck was a collar of sparkling diamonds.

'I simply couldn't move.

'Then the Swan spoke.

'She said, "Mortal. You have trespassed in my garden." Her voice was cold and went through me like steel. "Who are you? And how do you dare to steal from the Midnight Swan?"

'That was my chance. I should have explained, of course. Said sorry. Grovelled even, I suppose … but I was a very foolish young man. A little vain. Boastful. I have of course changed utterly since then.'

Seren nodded, solemn.

'So I drew myself up, rather haughtily, and said, "Madam Swan. I had no idea this was your garden. But I assure you, I am prepared to pay for the rose."

'It was a bad mistake.

'The Swan's head darted out at me. Its eyes were black with fury. "I don't sell my friends, mortal. But yes, you'll certainly pay for the rose. *With your life.*"

'I wanted to step back, but it was impossible. I couldn't move a muscle. The Swan heaved itself out of the water. It was enormous! It stood over me and spread its wings wide and they were so black! It was as if all the darkness in the world was in them. It stretched out its neck and hissed and all the other swans came and gathered about me in a terrible circle. I knew they would peck me to death in seconds so I shouted, "No! Wait. WAIT!"

'I had no idea really what I was saying. But my remarkable brain must have been working because I gasped, "Don't kill me! Let me bring you something instead! The thing you want most in all the world! Let me find it for you!"

'The Swan drew back. It tipped its head. Those eyes! So powerful and strange. And for a moment

I was sure I saw something else in them. A terrible sadness.

'The swans waited.

'I waited.

'Suddenly the black Swan waved the others away. When they had rustled back to the lake I breathed a huge gasp of relief. "What I want most?" the Swan snapped. "How do you know what that is?"

'"You can tell me, Majesty. Jewels, gold, anything, I can find them."

'It hissed a laugh of scorn. "A poor schoolmaster promising me such treasures." It put its black eyes very close to mine and I shivered. "I have jewels. I have gold. But yes. There is one thing I want more than anything in the world."

'"What?"

'"An Egg."

'"An egg?"

'"It was my only child, just ready to be born. It was snatched from my nest a thousand years ago by the Tylwyth Teg. I was a white swan then, generous and kind. Now I wear black as my mourning robe." She dipped her neck gracefully. "And I am no longer kind."

'I felt quite excited. This would save my life. "I'll find it for you! Just let me go and…"

"You have no idea what it would cost you to find. But this is what I'll do. I will let you live, but you'll live as a bird. And the spell will only be broken if you bring me what I want."

'Before I could even jump away, it had pecked my hand with its beak. A cold, icy pain went through me. I felt the strangest sensation. My skin split and cracked, my fingers became talons, my arm sprouted feathers. I stared down in horror and screeched but the Midnight Swan had slipped back into the lake and it was swimming away. It looked over its shoulder at me. All it said was, "Bring me the Egg. If you can."

'I opened my mouth to cry out but it was shaped all wrong and all I could say was *kek kek*. My body shrank. My bones hollowed. My limbs shrivelled. Cogs and wheels whirred in my chest. A key sprouted out and clicked in my side. I spread my arms and they were wings. And I flew, above the lake, over the garden wall, away. All the way home.'

He looked up. 'And that is how I came to be in this unfortunate situation.'

There was silence. Birdsong seemed to come back from a long distance. Seren said carefully, 'Thank you for telling us. It must have been … difficult.'

'I'm not proud of the episode,' the Crow muttered.

'The Egg of the Midnight Swan,' Tomos said. 'That's going to be tricky. If They have it…'

'Exactly.'

'So, did you try to find it?'

'Well, er … it's difficult. With Them. I tried to find the garden again but I have never been able to. Wherever it is, it's not in this world. So Enoch and I just went looking for cures.' It sank into a sudden morose heap of feathers. 'There aren't any of those; I know that now. I'm going to be like this for ever and ever. I just know it.'

Seren jumped up. 'No, you don't.' She went out of the summerhouse and sat on the steps, and the sun was hot on her face. 'Don't worry. We have that Box now. The Box of the Midnight Swan. It's got to help us.'

'A Box no one can open!' The Crow snorted. 'And if my superb intelligence can't work that problem out, how can a silly girl and a nosy boy help?'

'Hey,' Tomos objected. 'I'm not nosy.'

'You are.'

'I'm just interested.'

Seren hugged her knees. 'Don't worry about getting the Box open,' she said darkly. 'I'm on the case now and you know my methods, Watson. It will be … elementary.'

'Really? And how – exactly – do you mean to proceed?'

She had no idea. But she wasn't going to tell them that.

'You'll find out. Tomorrow.'

'What happened to the young lady?' Tomos asked suddenly, as if he had been thinking over the story. 'The one who asked for the rose?'

The Crow scowled. 'She married a farmer. And I dare say she deserved it.'

5

The green pen

Come to the party. Come to the Ball.
Come and see a girl not there at all.

Deep in dreams of a garden where roses sang sweet songs, Seren was woken by a sharp peck on her ear.

'*Ouch*.'

'Seren! Wake up!'

'Go away.' She rolled over sleepily and plunged back into a new dream of walking trees and talking snowflakes.

'Seren. Seren! Open your eyes at once!'

There was a horrible, insistent weight on her shoulder, then another peck, this time harder. It's *Them!* They're here!'

Her eyes snapped open. She sat up so suddenly that the Crow toppled off into a heap on the bedclothes.

'Where? Not inside the Plas!'

'No.' The Crow scrambled up, breathless. It held up a wing. 'Listen.'

She kept absolutely still.

'Hear that?'

It was a warm night, and her bedroom window was open. The room was shadowy. A few moths flitted and bumped against the dim ceiling.

'I can't…'

'There.'

Yes! She could hear it now! The softest and strangest of sounds. Like a swarm of bees far off.

'What is it?'

'Voices.' The Crow took off and swooped to the window. Its dark head was silhouetted against the panes. '*Their* voices.'

Seren slid out of bed and ran after it. She crouched down and peered cautiously over the sill. A bright shaft of moonlight glinted in on her fingers.

The lawns below were silvery, the trees masses of darkness. But there were lights. Small, eerie, greenish sparkles, hundreds of them, down by the lake.

'Glow worms,' the Crow sniffed. 'Cheap sort of magic.'

Among the lights, figures moved, shadows flickered.

'They're dancing,' Seren breathed.

Now she could almost hear the music, that beguiling faery music that made you tingle all over with fascination. It was so beautiful she wanted to stay there forever, but the Crow put both wings over her ears at once. 'Close the window!'

'But…'

'Do what I say, you silly girl!'

Scowling, Seren slammed the window down. At once the music stopped. The eerie lights vanished. The moonlit lawns of the lakeside were empty.

She felt empty too.

The Crow paced, agitated. 'I don't like this! Why are They celebrating? What's going on to make Them so happy? I mean, They don't need much excuse for singing and dancing but… Has anything unusual happened?'

'I don't think so.'

The Crow shook its head, unsatisfied. Its

jewel-bright eye glittered. 'Something's not right. There's trouble. I can smell it.'

Hopping to the door, he said, 'Come on. Bring a candle.'

Seren lit the candle hurriedly. Then she opened her bedroom door and peered out.

'Where are we going?'

'Downstairs.'

'But They can't get in…'

The Crow frowned. 'Well, something's giving me the shivers. Follow me. And keep quiet!'

Plas-y-Fran was sleeping peacefully. There was no fairy music here, no danger. The white corridor with its cabinets of china and old portraits stretched out into dimness, slanted by shafts of moonlight from the high windows.

The Crow swooped away. Sighing, Seren hurried after it. This was such a fuss over nothing! *They* were safely outside, and the house was guarded by all Denzil's horseshoes and hanging magic herbs. Everyone knew the Tylwyth Teg couldn't get past such a strong defence.

Then something Denzil said came back to her with a shiver.

Unless They were invited.

She ran silently after the Crow to the landing and crept down the main stairs, the bannister curving in the dimness under the portraits of long-dead Joneses. She glanced up at their pale faces, the ladies with hair piled high and the gentlemen with guns and dogs. They watched her go by. The Joneses were her family now. But sometimes she wondered if the people in the portraits were thinking *Who is that little girl in the nightdress? And why is she here, in our house?*

She bumped into a vase on a pedestal and grabbed it hastily before it fell.

The Crow tutted. 'What is the matter with you! Don't make so much noise!' It sniffed the air, turning its moth-eaten head this way and that. 'Definitely a whiff of spell somewhere. The library, maybe.'

They tiptoed over the dark creaky floorboards. At the library door Seren turned the handle and opened the door a tiny crack. She peeped in.

Everything seemed to be quiet, so she slid inside. The Crow flapped after her.

The huge bookshelves reached up to the ceiling, their gilt spines enticing; all their enchanting volumes of story closed and asleep.

But the curtains, usually shut tight at night, were drawn back, so that moonlight lit the room. Seren held the candle up, though she hardly needed it. And then she saw something impossible.

On the table in the centre of the room a green pen was writing.

All by itself!

It was scribbling elegant names on a pile of cream stationary. Seren recognised the gold letters of Lady Mair's invitations. The invitations to the Midsummer Ball!

'What on earth…!' the Crow gasped.

As if it heard, the pen gave a jump and scribbled faster. They saw that as each invitation was written it folded itself up and became a creamy paper bat. Hundreds of them were flitting out of the window, an outpouring of invitations.

The Crow gave a squawk of horror.

'Get that pen! NOW!'

Seren had to put the candle down carefully but then she made a dive at the table. The pen leapt into the air, ink splashing from the open inkwell; it dived under the pile of papers but Seren flung them aside and grabbed it, feeling the greenness of it squirm in her fingers.

'My goodness.' The Crow soared over the desk. 'This is dreadful! This is a disaster!'

It was diving and flapping furiously at the invitations but there were too many and even as it snatched one and tore it to shreds dozens of others were streaming out of the window in a great long line. The Crow skidded to a halt on the sill and stared up at them hopelessly. Then a crafty glint came into its eye.

'Hold tight! This will be uncomfortable!' It took a breath and spoke a sentence. It sounded like a poem said backwards.

At once Seren felt all the air had been sucked out of her lungs. She had to gasp for breath. Her dressing gown turned inside out by itself and then back again. Her hair lifted and tingled round her scalp. All the doors in the room, even the smallest cupboards, opened and closed with a sudden clap!

The invitations shrivelled.

They turned black and rained from the ceiling like cinders.

The green pen gave a hopeless shiver. Then Seren realised she was holding nothing but green dust that seeped through her fingers onto the desk, with a gold trickle where the nib had been.

'Got them!' the Crow snapped, triumphantly. 'HA!'

Seren sat breathlessly on the chair. 'That was … amazing.' She opened her fingers. The green dust powdered down onto the paper. 'What is it? Dried leaves?'

'Who knows. Who cares!' The Crow paraded haughtily up and down the desk, leaving inky footprints on the paper and kicking invitations out of its way. 'Whatever it was it couldn't get the better of me! Did you *see* that! One word, one imperious command and BANG! Gone! Obliterated. DESTROYED!'

'Yes,' Seren said, 'but…'

'I mean, there's not another person in Wales who could even come close. Not even that wizard down in Carmarthen. Or that wise woman in Bangor with the black cat who thinks she's so…'

'The pen was writing invitations,' Seren said, in a very small voice. 'And who knows how many it had already sent out.'

The Crow stopped in mid-stride. It swivelled its head and looked at her and for a moment they shared a look of horror.

The Crow groaned. 'The Midsummer Ball! They will get in!'

Seren got up and ran to the window. 'Can't we stop it somehow?'

'It's too late! Who brought that wretched faery pen into the house? What IDIOT...'

'Tomos. He thought it was Lady Mair's. It's not his fault.'

The Crow huffed and kek-kekked and stomped around the table. 'Well, the fat's in the fire now. We can't stop Them coming. I...'

Seren jumped up. 'Listen!'

Footsteps in the corridor.

Instantly, she dived under the desk. The Crow stood rigid by the inkwell.

The door opened and Mrs Villiers swept in carrying an oil lamp.

The housekeeper wore a long frilly blue dressing gown and her hair was curled in rags. Seren stifled a snort of laughter, and crouched lower, because if she was found how could she explain?

Mrs Villiers took a quick look around. She went to the window and closed it.

Then a voice said, 'Mrs Villiers? Are you still up?'

She turned. 'Oh, Captain. I was actually in my room but it's so hot, and I was sure I heard a noise down here. A banging, like doors. Just as well, as someone seems to have left a candle alight. Goodness, how dangerous, with all these books.' She blew it out quickly.

Captain Jones came in. He wore a dressing gown, too, and had a large book under his arm. 'Well, there's no one here now. Perhaps you should close the window, though, even though the night is so warm.'

'I'll do that. Better safe than sorry.' She hurried over. 'Strange. It's already closed.'

Then she gave a gasp, and Seren knew she had seen the inky stains on the desk.

'Oh heavens! Look at all this mess. A bird must have got in.' She squinted at the inkwell, the scattered papers, the rigid Crow and the brass model of Llandaff Cathedral next to it. 'And these ornaments really do need a dusting. Look at them!' She wiped a smear of dust off the Crow's head with one finger. 'Disgusting. I shall certainly speak to Lily about it. That girl is shirking her duties!'

Seren kept perfectly still. She could see the Crow wobbling. He must be furious! What if he said something! She prayed he would keep his temper.

'Yes, well. Good night.' Captain Jones turned to the door. Then, a little doubtfully, he stopped and turned back. 'Mrs Villiers, may I ask you a rather serious question. In confidence?'

Mrs Villiers straightened. 'Of course, sir.'

'What is your opinion – and I would like your honest opinion, if you please – of Seren?'

Seren's eyes went wide with astonishment.

Mrs Villiers seemed startled too. '*Seren*! Goodness… Why she's a dear. Though of course, when she first came … when things were so difficult, and dear Master Tomos was missing…'

Captain Jones nodded impatiently.

'…well, I confess, I was rather unsure about her even being here. An orphan, you know. And she was so dirty and cheeky at first.'

'I was not!' Seren muttered, furious. Never mind the Crow, *she* wanted to burst out in temper. But Mrs Villiers hadn't finished. 'But now? Oh Captain Jones, she is so sensible and generous! A little wild at times, a little bold in her ideas. Far too many sensational books, of course. But well … such a sweet girl…'

Seren's fury disappeared abruptly. Gosh. That was all right. Who would have thought stiff old Mrs V would say that.

But Captain Jones didn't seem quite satisfied. 'Yes, but … do you truly think she is a suitable companion for Tomos?'

Mrs Villiers folded her hands together. 'Oh sir, that's not for me to say. You and Lady Mair have been so kind that… There is nothing wrong about Seren, sir, I hope?'

'Well, not quite wrong…' Captain Jones shuffled awkwardly. 'You see it's just that…'

Seren edged a fraction nearer, desperate to hear. As she did so her hand slid on the polished floor and the planks creaked, sharply.

Captain Jones turned at once. 'What on earth was that?'

He hurried towards the desk.

Seren froze.

She couldn't move!

Her heart thudded and she went cold all over. Captain Jones' slippered feet came right up to the desk. She saw his knees.

He was bending down.

His face was staring right at her.

Their eyes met.

It was a moment of nightmare.

Seren swallowed. She opened her mouth to say something, anything, but somehow she couldn't manage a word and at the very same moment Captain Jones blinked and shook his head, puzzled. 'Nothing here. Must have just been the floorboards relaxing.'

He scrambled back, leaving Seren staring at the darkness in amazement.

He must have seen her.

Why hadn't he said anything?

She was so baffled she only realised they had both gone when their voices faded and the door closed with a click.

The library was dark and silent for a whole minute.

Then the Crow snapped. 'That *presumptuous* woman! How dare she call me disgusting! If I don't turn her into a worm…'

Seren scrambled out. 'He saw me! He looked right at me!'

'Ah, but he didn't see you.' The Crow looked smug. 'I made sure of that. It was an extremely tricky feat of magic.'

'You mean I was invisible?' She stared down at her hands and nightgown and feet. 'Oh my goodness! How can I still see myself?'

'No! Invisible! What does that even mean? He didn't see you. I convinced him there was nothing there. His eyes were working all right and you were actually there but he didn't believe it. Call it a sort of hypnotism.' The Crow flapped down and strode to the door. It seemed immensely pleased with itself. 'Ha! Superb timing. Had to hold it just so… Another thing no one else could have done with such … panache.'

'No,' Seren said. 'Thank you.'

'Now you'd better get back to bed in case they come back.' The Crow turned. 'What's wrong?'

She frowned. She wanted to say *Why was Captain Jones asking about me like that?* but the Crow would have just shrugged that off so instead she said, 'You've forgotten the invitations.'

Instantly the Crow groaned. 'Another problem to sort out.' It yawned. 'And after those two electrifying spells I'm feeling way too tired to think.'

An hour later, curled up in the dark bed, Seren lay worrying. Everything seemed to be going wrong. She had to be very careful. Behave really well. Not get in anyone's way. Not read too many books. There was a deep small cold fear inside her that wouldn't go away, and for a moment she let herself imagine the journey in the train back to the orphanage, and the doors opening and her small self walking in, down the double row of girls sitting at supper, and all of them turning to look at her and laughing.

She shivered, and turned over. That was a nightmare she didn't intend to happen.

Fiercely she told herself not to worry.

Tomorrow she would get things sorted things out.

Tomorrow.

Starting with the Box.

6

Ask it politely

Cross words never
make things better.

But by twelve o'clock the next morning she was leaning her head on her arms, thoroughly annoyed and irritated. 'I give UP! This is hopeless! What else can we do?'

The Box lay on the table, surrounded by all the tools they had used to try to open it. Paper knives and penknives. Scissors and saws. Screwdrivers and letter slitters.

On the sofa by the fireplace the Crow lay on its back, giving the faintest of moans. 'Don't ask me. I've used every spell I know. I'm EXHAUSTED.'

They had completely run out of ideas, and

there was the Box with its starry lid sealed as tightly shut as ever. And still no sign of the Swan on its lid.

Far off, the kitchen bell rang.

'Lunch!' Tomos jumped up. 'Oh and it's parsnip soup today. Come on, Seren. Let's go!'

Seren was only too glad to scramble after him, but the Crow glowered and sank deeper into its feathers.

'Parsnip soup! How lovely – for some! With scones, no doubt. CHEESE scones.'

'We won't be long, honestly,' Seren said, from the door.

'Take all the time you want.' The Crow pecked viciously at the Box. 'I'm going absolutely nowhere!'

Seren had hoped for a peaceful time to think about things, but in the kitchen it was incredibly hot and busy, even with all the windows open. Two extra cooks had been brought in to help with preparations for the Ball and all the other servants were working hard too. Dough was being rolled out, chickens plucked and cakes baked. Gwyn was carrying a high pile of vegetables backwards through the door. He dumped them in the pantry and waved at Seren.

'Come and eat now, with Seren and Master Tomos,' Mrs Villiers snapped. 'But first wash your hands.'

A small table was laid for them in the corner, out of the bustle. Denzil sat there already, sipping an enormous mug of tea, and smoking his small clay pipe.

For a while Seren, Tomos and Gwyn just ate. Then, when she was comfortably full, Seren said, 'Denzil. Listen. Something's happened.'

They all looked at her.

'Due to an … um … unfortunate mistake, some extra invitations were written. To um, well, to *Them*.'

Tomos said, 'What?' and Gwyn muttered something she didn't understand in Welsh. They both looked dismayed, but not as much as Denzil.

The small man stared at her. His silence was scary. He took his pipe out and looked down at it. 'This is bad, girl. Very bad. How did it happen?'

'Well, like I said, it was a mistake.' Seren caught Tomos's eye – she didn't want to get him into trouble for bringing the green pen into the house. 'It was no one's fault, and we are going to try to stop Them, honestly, if we can.'

'How?'

'Well, we have a Box … only, Denzil, if you had a thing that wouldn't open, that wouldn't do what you wanted, however much you tried to make it, what would you do?'

'An enchanted thing?' Denzil said sharply.

'Yes.'

'You be careful, Seren bach.'

'We are careful. And it's not just me and Tomos. A friend is helping us. A feathered friend, if you know what I mean.'

'Mmm.' Denzil puffed at his pipe. Then he knocked a dottle of tobacco from it onto the edge of the table. 'Your schoolmaster. I know him.'

Seren nodded. She was never sure how much Denzil knew about the Crow. Though actually, she thought, there wasn't much that Denzil didn't know about what went on in Plas-y-Fran. Suddenly she wanted to know if Captain Jones had asked him any questions about her, but it was too late. As he stood and picked up his plate he murmured something so quietly that only she could hear over the clash and clatter of pans.

'As for your Box, I would ask it.'

'Ask it?'

Denzil leaned closer. 'An enchanted object needs to have respect shown it, bach. So yes, I would ask it, politely, to open itself, if I was you.'

Why hadn't she thought of that?

Dumping her spoon in the dish, and leaving Gwyn and Tomos staring, she ran.

In the schoolroom the Crow was perched on the globe. It shrugged haughtily. 'Well, if you think the opinion of a mere servant is better than mine, go ahead.'

'Denzil is not a mere servant. I'm going to try it.'

She stood looking down at the Box, her hands on the starry cover. Then she said, 'Box of the Midnight Swan, listen to me. We're really sorry we've been trying to force you open. It's up to you. But it would be really nice if you let us see what's inside you. Please.'

Nothing happened.

Tomos hurtled in through the door. 'What…?'

The Crow held up a wing, then folded it, smug. 'Seren has some ridiculous idea that…'

The Box exploded.

That was the only word for it. It burst open

with an enormous crash. All sorts of things were flung out, smacking against the walls and ceiling.

Seren ducked; Tomos screeched.

The Crow stared.

Flowers and bees, sugar almonds and gingerbread. Swallows and swifts and a squirrel that scampered straight out of the window and up a tree. A glorious sweet-smelling fountain of thousands of petals and seeds that surged up to the ceiling and pattered down on tables and chairs and floor all over the room like crimson rain.

Seren watched, wide-eyed.

Slowly, everything fell and settled.

When the last petal had drifted down she took her arms off her head and stood up again.

'Gosh,' she said. And then, to the Box, 'Thanks.'

The schoolroom was transformed. It was as scented as a beautiful garden and carpeted with petals. On the table, the Box lay open, its lid wide.

The Crow scrambled over hastily. 'Good work, Seren.' It looked inside.

'Ah,' it said.

Seren and Tomos ran to see. For a few moments they both stood there silent.

Then Seren said the obvious.

'It's empty.'

She was so disappointed!

Hastily the Crow put its head right inside and looked in every corner. 'There must be more than this. There has to be!'

Actually Seren thought, it wasn't quite empty. There was a cushioned interior of pale blue silk. It was a large empty padded space. And the space was egg-shaped.

'It's to hold the Swan's Egg,' she said, understanding. 'That's all. That's Her heart's desire after all, and that makes it yours, too.'

'Well, it's absolutely no use to me!' the Crow snapped. He sounded bitterly annoyed. 'And you saying it would help!'

'It's not my fault!' Seren frowned. 'Well, at least when we find the Egg we have something safe to put it in.'

'Find it! HA! You have no idea…!'

'He's right, Seren.' Tomos shook his head sadly. 'It doesn't help him get his human shape back.'

'Not only that.' The Crow was acid. '*They* gave you this Box. *They* played a trick on you … and you fell for it. No wonder all those goblin faces were laughing. They must think you such a silly girl!'

Seren went red. She felt so upset she wanted to cry. 'You're wrong,' she snapped. 'I stole it. And anyway, how hard did you actually try to find the Egg?'

'Very hard.'

'Are you sure?'

'Tried for a hundred years,' the Crow said huffily.

Seren shook her head. 'You've always been scared of Them…'

'Never!'

'I mean They captured you and put you in a cage. They want you…'

'Of course. Who wouldn't? But…'

'Did you ever go into Their country?'

The Crow was silent. Then it muttered, 'Of course not. Do I look totally mad?'

Tomos groaned.

Seren said, 'But that's what we need to do! Go and see Them. Ask Them…'

'Pointless.' The Crow hopped down into the carpet of petals and turned its back. 'Besides I would NEVER lower myself to beg!'

'Then you're far too proud, and you deserve to be a Crow for ever!' She was so angry she turned her back too. He was so infuriating!

There was an awkward silence.

Birds sang outside in the hot shimmer of the air. Bees hummed in the lavender.

A few petals rose from the floor and drifted back down again.

Tomos said, 'Stop arguing, you two. It won't get us anywhere.'

'Well, that's all right because HE doesn't want to go anywhere,' Seren said. She felt really annoyed and wanted to scream but it wasn't just about the Crow and the Box. It was because she didn't know what was going to happen to her, and she was scared.

'Tell HER,' the Crow said loftily, 'that only fools go into Their country. I'm far too wise.'

'Tell HIM,' Seren snapped, 'that he's not worth bothering with.'

'Tell HER,' the Crow said, 'that anyone who thinks they are Sherlock Holmes is too silly to help.'

'Tell HIM,' Seren gasped, 'that at least I'm not scared of Them.'

Suddenly she grabbed the Box and marched to the door with it. 'And I'm not silly. And if HE doesn't want my help, then HE won't get it. GOODBYE.'

She marched out with her head high and along the corridor to her room. Once there she slammed the door with the loudest slam she could make, threw the Box onto the bed and herself after it. She was furious!

She lay with her chin on her hands looking towards the open window.

Slowly she calmed down.

It was very hot.

That was part of the trouble.

The window was wide and the sky beyond it was a deep, deep blue, as if it went on for ever.

You could never see the sky in the orphanage. The windows had always been tiny, and high up in the walls, and when no one was looking you had to grab with your hands and tug yourself up just to get your chin over the sill.

Seren shook her head. She hated remembering the orphanage and she wasn't going to. And she wasn't going back there either.

But maybe it would be a school.

What would that be like?

'If I don't like it,' she said aloud, 'I can just run away.'

Outside, swallows flitted, catching flies on the

wing. Suddenly she scrambled up and ran to the window and looked across the lawns at the lake. There were always birds on there; now she saw geese and out on the water, swans. They had cygnets with them, a small line of five grey shapes sailing along behind their parents. So she couldn't even steal a swan's egg. Not that she would have done that.

Sadly she leaned her head against the side of the window.

The Crow was such an irritating creature!

There was a small tittering sound. She glanced up and saw that the line of starlings on the roof of the house had got longer. There must be forty or fifty of them now. They were watching the preparations for the Ball.

Some of the maids were carrying out huge red lanterns; Gwyn was up a tree stringing the lanterns from the branches. There were tents on the lawn, too, and tables inside ready for food and drink.

The smell of freshly cut grass rose to her.

Gwyn waved.

She waved back.

When the last lantern was up he climbed down and came and stood under her window.

'What's the matter, Seren? Beth sy'n bod?'

'Nothing.'

He shook his head. 'I can tell. You're cross.'

'Well, maybe. But I can't explain. There's something I have to find and I don't know how to find it and it's the Ball tonight and I'm worried … about Them.'

'So is Denzil.'

For a moment they watched Lily and Sian carry out tables and set them up. Then Seren said, 'Gwyn, where would I find a swan's egg?'

He stared. 'It's too late to find one. They've all hatched.'

'I know. That's the problem.'

'Gwyn!' Mrs Villiers was beckoning. 'I need you to go to the village. Right now.'

'Sorry, Seren.' He backed away. 'If you'd looked a few months ago there were some. You'd need magic to find one now.'

'Yes,' she said.

Then he was running to the stables.

She pulled her head in and stared at the reflection of the Box in the dressing-table window.

She didn't have magic.

But They did.

And she wasn't scared of Them.

7

A promise is made

You may be bold, and merry and bright.
But we are the fears that come out at night.

It was very dangerous, but she was sure she could do it.

First, she went down to the cellars and tried the locked door, but she already knew this way was blocked; Denzil had made sure of that. No one would be going down the strange golden stairs as Tomos once had. She had to find Them by another way.

She had the Box in a small bag hanging over her shoulder. It clunked against her hip.

She crept out of the side door just before Mrs Villiers could see her and ran down the path past the greenhouses and the kitchen garden with its rows of cabbages and carrots, then slipped through the gate. The hanging iron implements rattled ominously as she closed the latch behind her. Now she was outside.

They could be anywhere here.

The wood was the best place to start, she thought. In woods you always felt as if They were watching you, from behind trees and up in branches.

Seren walked across the lawn. It was very hot; she was glad to get into the shade of the trees and under the heavy canopy of branches. They were so thick with summer growth that soon she couldn't see anything around her but leaves. The path grew thin and spindly, and the trunks of the trees seemed closer together than usual.

She walked on.

It was a cooler, greener world here and she was deep inside it. And maybe she was already in Their world, because she had walked so far that she should surely have come to the wall of the estate by now. Instead, the day felt sleepy and strange.

Bright butterflies danced around her.

And she felt the ground was rising, and she was climbing, and that shouldn't be, because the park was flat.

Then the sounds began. Creaks and rustles.

Murmurs and whispers.

She looked back, and spun around trying to catch a movement. There was nothing, but she knew They were here.

She walked on boldly until she came into a small clearing in the trees, where she stopped.

This was the place. She could feel Their curiosity and laughter and malice.

She looked all around. Then she took a breath and said in a loud voice, 'You stole an Egg from the Midnight Swan. I know all about that. It was very wrong to do that. So now I'm asking you to give me the Egg. We need it very much. I would be very grateful.' To be polite she added, 'Thank you.'

In the silence that followed she shivered a little.

Really she shouldn't have come here like this.

The Crow would be even more furious when he found out.

She could feel in her bones how dangerous it was.

She was just about to turn and run back as fast

as she could when the soft voice came from the leaves to her right. *'If we do, what will you give us in return?'*

Seren's heart jumped.

'What do you want?' she asked, turning.

'What we always want.' The voice came from behind her now, silvery and close. *'A human child.'*

Seren realised that she was not surprised. She had sort of known this would happen.

'You can't have Tomos,' she said, very firmly. 'I don't think that's right.'

'Then we will have you, bright Star.'

The voice was on the other side of her now. Or was it more than one voice? She turned, trying to see *Them*, but only the leaves quivered. Were there faces in there, and eyes, and fingers? Were those emeralds and gold glinting, or just sparkles of sunlight?

She was very scared. 'I'm not at all sure about that. I'll have to see...'

'You must promise to give us what we want. Or we keep the Swan's Egg.'

She blew out her cheeks and clutched her hands into fists. The Tylwyth Teg were clever. They knew she had no choice. Well, she did, actually, she could turn and walk away. But then the Crow would be trapped in the body of a clockwork bird for ever. And then she had a strange thought: that living with Them had to be better than the orphanage.

She wasn't sure she believed that but suddenly she felt reckless. 'All right. Give me the Egg and I'll come in return. That is, if you still want me to.'

As soon as she'd said it she felt cold and shivery with dread. Around her a great excited whispering and twittering and humming broke out, and the trees stirred, as if hundreds of beings were moving in the branches. Music began playing, playful and far off.

'*That's good. We are very pleased.*'

'So I can have the Egg?'

She wondered if it would somehow fall at her feet.

'*You have to go up and get it. It's not far.*'

A small dark opening appeared in the greenery. She saw the leaves were pulled aside by strange, silvery hands.

She walked towards the gap, and as she went through it a whisper tickled her ear.

'*At the Midsummer Ball, bright Star. We will*

*come for you when the moon is full. When the
night is shortest. When the roses are in bloom. We
will not forget. You belong to us now.'*

Then she was in a dark and narrow corridor of
tangled branches. She hurried along, ducking
down so that her hair didn't get caught, and trying
not to think at all about what she had done.

Soon the branches were so low she had to go
down on hands and knees in the litter, and her
fingers sank deep into it, as if thousands of years
of leaves had fallen and died in here.

Then, just when her face was almost on the
floor, she realised there was room to stand up, so
she did. She was in a green, dim space in the
wood.

In front of her was a hollow tree.

It had been an oak once, enormous and
ancient. Maybe lightning had blasted it, long ago,
because now the inside was just a ridged and
knotted emptiness.

Seren walked all around the tree. She looked
up.

She had to put her head so far back it made her
giddy, but there was a knotted mesh of branches
up there, and high in the branches, so high it was

scary, there was a nest. It was made of odd shiny things, as far as she could see. She realised what she had to do. The Egg must be in that nest, and she had to climb up and get it.

For a moment, as she hesitated, she almost thought she heard voices calling her name urgently, very faint and far away. It might have been Tomos, or the Crow. Perhaps they were looking for her. If they found her they would tell her to stop, so she slipped inside the hollow trunk of the oak, put her hands up and her foot on the twisty roots and began to climb.

It was not too difficult, rather more as if the tree had a winding staircase inside it. There were ridges of old timber, and gnarls and knots and branches to catch hold of and pull herself higher. Soon swallows and swifts circled round her. She climbed carefully past a nest of bees that buzzed in her face, through a tangle of ivy that caught in her hair. Slants of sunlight dazzled her eyes. A squirrel watched her and a hawk flew away with a flap of wings.

Soon she was breathless and her heart was thumping, but she went on, and up. Now the stairway was very tight and it was made of smaller branches that bent under her weight as if she was coming to the top. Then her head came out through a crown of leaves, and she could see for miles.

She held on tight, and stared. What a strange country it was!

Not Wales at all. Not anywhere she knew.

Great mountains surrounded it, all glassy and snow-covered. Vast unbroken forests stretched forever. And over there she could see the sea! A green, shifting ocean far in the distance, but how could that be?

Plas-y-Fran was nowhere to be seen.

This was a different world altogether.

'Gosh,' she said, clutching as the branches swayed.

It was too strange to think about, really, so she shifted her weight and took a breath of the cold fresh air. Then she struggled around with her back to the tree trunk, and saw the nest.

It was made of gold. She knew that at once, because it shone so brightly. It was out on a thick branch, a good way out from the main trunk. Suddenly she realised what a long way down the ground was.

'Don't look down, silly,' she told herself.

She got down on her hands and knees and began to crawl along the thick bough. It was scary, but she kept her eyes on the nest. As she pulled herself nearer she saw that it was made of a mass of objects, all shinily woven together. Cups and plates and knives and forks. Salvers and necklaces, dishes and rings and winding watch chains. Amulets and bracelets and tiaras. And hundreds of coins, all glinting and shining among the branches.

Seren was almost blinded by the splendour of it. It was a heap of treasure!

But there was no mistaking the Egg.

It sat right in the middle of the heap. It was large and smooth and creamy white, with no markings on it at all. She thought it was bigger than a normal swan's egg; in any case it would be awkward enough to get down. The Egg of the Midnight Swan! What if she dropped it! She dared not even think about that.

Seren crawled nearer. With every movement the branch dipped. It was really springy now, and her hands were green with lichen and her knees were sore. Finally, she lifted one hand and reached out. She had to stretch, because she didn't dare let go with her other hand. Her fingers waved in the air.

Not quite enough.

She slid a tiny bit more.

A bee buzzed round her. She ducked away, and wobbled. 'Stop that,' she hissed.

She touched the Egg.

It moved slightly. She jerked her hand back, because she had to be so careful!

Then, with her knees and ankles gripping tight, she let go of the branch, waited till she felt balanced, and bent and lifted the Egg with both hands.

A chill breeze gusted around her.

She wobbled.

Quickly she wrapped the Egg in her skirt and held it there with one hand.

She started to slide backwards. It was very difficult. What made it worse was that a wind seemed to have arrived from nowhere, and the branches were bending and flexing and her hair was blowing in her eyes. But finally she felt the tree trunk at her back.

She grabbed the trunk and held it tight.

For a moment she felt so breathless she couldn't move. How could she climb down? Holding an

Egg? It would be impossible! If only the Crow was here!

Yes, but that's your fault, she told herself sternly. Because you didn't tell him where you were going. And so now you are going to have to do this on your own.

She nodded.

And then laughed at herself.

The Box! This was just what it was for!

She wriggled the bag round and balanced the Egg between her knees. Then she pulled the Box out and opened it, and there was the beautiful egg-shaped space, all waiting. She laid the Egg in its pale blue silk and closed the Box tight.

She almost felt it sigh with satisfaction.

The wind gusted. The tree shook.

The Box wobbled.

'No… *Wait*…! 'Seren grabbed at it. She slipped. She screamed and quite suddenly everything went giddy and the world skewed and she was hanging upside down from her arms and feet, clinging on tight. And there, flashing past her, down and down and crashing through the branches below, she heard the Box fall all the way to the floor.

8

A warning is given

Magic is made of simple things.
A mirror, a crystal, a pad of pins.

Seren kept her eyes closed. She didn't want to see. But her arms were aching and she would fall if she didn't do something, so she swung her way to the branch and climbed back up onto it, her boots wedged in cracks, her green hands slipping and sliding on moss and lichen.

Once she was the right way up, she took a deep breath and wriggled to the trunk. Then she hurried down.

After the first really wobbly steps it wasn't so bad. Soon she was inside the tree and scrambling down the wooden steps, twisting and turning into the dark faster than was safe, racing down until, quite suddenly, she burst out onto the forest floor.

She looked round, gasping.

The Box lay on its side in a heap of leaves.

It was quite intact.

There was no sight or sound of Them.

But she knew they were probably watching.

She picked it up quickly and opened it and YES, there it was. She had been terrified it would be a mess of yolk and shell but it must be really strong.

Was there a crack?

She couldn't tell in the dim green light. She shoved it in the bag and ran.

The way back through the tangled trees seemed shorter than before; in minutes she was in a more normal woodland, and it was hot, with shafts of sun all around her, and then she was out and running towards the lake and there was Plas-y-Fran in front of her, all its old stone golden and shining in the sun.

She stopped, breathless.

She had done it!

'You've done WHAT!'

The Crow was perched on the soldiers' fort in Tomos's room of toys.

He stared at the Egg as if he couldn't believe his eyes. He spluttered and gulped. 'Its... Well ... it can't possibly... How...? I don't... Goodness!'

Seren sat wearily on the chair by the table. She felt rather tired.

'Seren, it's fantastic! You were so brave!' Tomos stared at the Egg, fascinated. He put out a finger towards it and the Crow almost screamed.

'NO! Be careful! It's so precious! If indeed it is the right one...'

'It is,' Seren said. 'I got it from Them.'

The Crow blinked one jewel-bright eye sideways at her. Then it hopped closer. 'From Them?'

Seren nodded. She was rather dreading what was coming.

'But how did you get it? I mean They wouldn't just give it you,' Tomos said.

'I ... er ... sort of asked Them for it.'

The Crow emitted a terrible groan.

'And They just said yes?' Tomos asked.

Seren raised her eyebrows. 'Well...'

'*NO*,' the Crow said. 'No! I'm not having this!' It

shook its head so hard feathers flew out. 'I've told you a hundred times you never NEVER make requests of Them! They always want something in return, and there are two things They like best – as you well know – one is treasure and the other is a human child. So, please tell me, you foolish, foolish, *foolish* girl, that you didn't make Them any sort of promise.'

Seren felt unhappy. She didn't think she had ever seen the Crow so upset. She said quietly, 'Just a very little one. Nothing at all really. It's just … I had to do something. And I'm sorry we argued and that I said you deserved to be a clockwork bird. That was a nasty thing to say.'

The Crow drew itself up with dignity. 'I'm sorry, too. I'm afraid it has led to a most dangerous situation.'

'But aren't you glad to have the Egg?' Tomos jumped up. 'I mean we can take it straight to the Swan and she will give you back your human shape and everything will be all right! That's good, isn't it?'

The Crow was silent. Then he nodded heavily. 'Let's hope so. Dear me, let's hope so.' He glanced at Seren sideways and she knew he was deeply worried. 'Let's hope we haven't paid too high a price.' Then he preened a feather thoughtfully. 'Right. We leave at once. We need to be back by midnight. Tomos, you'll bring the Box. And I also want three other things.'

'What?' Tomos breathed. 'A sword? A compass?'

'Silly boy. Those things are useless where we're going. I want a mirror, a small glass pyramid…'

Tomos stared. 'They don't sound very useful.'

'You know nothing about magic.'

'What's the third?'

The Crow looked at him sly and sideways.

'A pin-cushion. Full of pins.'

Seren raced upstairs to wash her green hands and face.

Plas-y-Fran felt strange. The corridors were shivery and excited. All the windows were wide open, and little gusts of warm breezes lifted the gauzy curtains and creaked the doors.

As she passed the drawing room she saw it was beautifully dressed for the Midsummer Ball.

Hangings of yellow silk and blue damask drifted. All the paintings had been dusted and their gilt frames shone. Huge bunches of flowers –

lavender and phlox and night-scented stock –
stood in glass vases and perfumed the air. As she
raced by, her small reflection flickered in polished
furniture and mirrors and shiny cabinets.

She washed at top speed, pulled on clean boots
and raced back down again, but as she hurtled
past the side table in the hall a large letter in the
tray caught her eye.

She stopped dead.

Then she went closer.

It was a creamy, heavy-looking envelope, thick
with paper. It was addressed to *Captain Jones,
Plas-y-Fran, Urgent and Personal.* In the bottom
right hand corner the sender's name was printed.

G.R. FREEMAN
Solicitor At Law
Staple Inn
London

Seren's heart gave a leap. That had been her aunt's
lawyer. Why was he writing to Captain Jones? Was
it about her?

Her hand crept towards the envelope but at that
moment Mrs Villiers bustled out of the drawing

room, her arms full of flowers. 'Seren! Don't touch anything! Everything is ready for the Ball. The first guests are expected in a few hours. Some are staying the night, you know.'

Seren jumped back. 'Are they?'

'You and Tomos will have supper in the schoolroom, and then you can come down when the music starts. Meanwhile, stay out of the way.'

Seren nodded. She started to hurry to the door. Then she turned, abruptly. 'Thank you, Mrs Villiers.'

'Goodness. What for?'

'For everything. Since I came.'

'Well … I… That's quite all right, Seren. Quite all right.' Mrs Villiers seemed a little embarrassed. She hastily arranged the flowers in a vase.

'Off you go now. No arguing.'

She swept up the envelope and carried it quickly away towards the Captain's study.

Seren frowned. She walked slowly down the steps.

Outside, the summer afternoon was waning. The stable clock struck four. Tomos was jigging with impatience. 'Come on! It's time to go!'

He had a small knapsack on his back. 'The Box

is in here. And the other stuff.' He whispered. 'Let's go. '

'Where's the Crow?'

'Waiting outside.'

They flitted through the busy house. Everyone was so caught up in preparations that even Lady Mair didn't notice them slip past the dining-room door, where she was inspecting the table.

On the terrace Seren hissed, 'Where are you?'

'Here.' The Crow was a dark shape perched on the low stone wall. 'Got everything?'

'Yes.'

'Sure?'

'Yes!'

'Well, let me see.'

Tomos opened the bag; the Crow peered in and rummaged. 'Good. Now. We go fast and silent. And remember. This is a journey into a very strange place. Keep your wits about you. Don't speak unless I tell you to. For heaven's sake, don't touch anything. And don't,' it glared at Seren, '*promise anything*!'

'I won't.' She felt a little annoyed, but excited too.

The Crow flew. They hurried after it over the musky warmth of the summer lawns.

But just as they got to the gate into the park a small figure stepped out of the bushes in front of them and said, 'You wait right there.'

Seren gasped. The Crow screeched to a halt. Tomos almost fell over.

Denzil said, 'Where are you off to?'

He had the shotgun over his arm.

'What are you doing with that?' Seren stared.

'Keeping an eye, bach, just keeping an eye.' The small man looked at the Crow. 'So. The time has come, has it? I think it's about time we spoke, Sir, you and I.'

'Yes.' The Crow nodded. 'Perhaps it is.'

There was another stir of branches and Seren saw Gwyn standing in the bushes behind, staring wide-eyed at the Crow.

'Because I am not allowing Master Tomos and Miss Seren to be taken away anywhere,' Denzil said firmly.

'He's not taking us, Denzil…' Tomos began, but the Crow held up a wing to silence him.

'You have no need to concern yourself, my man,' the Crow said loftily. 'I am highly experienced in magical matters, I can assure you, and…'

'Assure all you like, sir.' Denzil stood, stockily unmoved. 'They will not be going anywhere unless I think it is safe.'

'Please, Denzil!' Seren stepped forward. 'I haven't got time to explain everything now but it's really important we go! It's to get the Crow back to his proper shape. We've got everything we need and we shouldn't be in danger...'

'There is always danger meddling with the faery people.' Denzil shook his dark head. 'You know that, Sir.'

'I do.' The Crow looked down its beak. 'But let me tell you that this ... disguise ... is not who I actually am. In fact, I am a prince ... well, professor ... or rather...' It caught Seren's eye and cleared its throat guiltily. '...well, a schoolteacher. I am, Sir, a schoolteacher and so am well used to looking after children.' Suddenly, it looked crestfallen, and its voice went small. 'I'm not just a moth-eaten toy. Please don't think that.'

'I'm thinking you are much more than you seem. So maybe you should go alone.'

'Er ... unfortunately ... due to my present position ... well, shape ... I am unable to carry the Egg.'

'Egg?' Gwyn whispered.

'Listen.' Seren was impatient. 'We'll be back by midnight. *I promise*! We have to go with him, Denzil, because he can't do it by himself, and you have to stay here and guard the house because They will be coming to the Ball...'

The small man sighed heavily. 'Indeed, Seren bach, I know that.'

'Please, Denzil! Please trust me.'

For a long moment Denzil stood silent. Then he said, 'If you are not back, Seren, if the Captain thinks you have run off and taken Tomos with you into danger, he will no longer want you here. Do you really want to risk all that you have at Plas-y-Fran for a stranger?'

Seren bit her lip. 'The Crow's not a stranger. I have to take the risk.'

'Anyway,' Tomos said stoutly. 'I'm not being taken. I'm going because I want to.'

'Very well.' Denzil looked at the Crow and the Crow looked back at him. Finally he stepped forward. They were beak to nose. He nodded. 'All right. But listen to me, Master Schoolmaster. If anything happens to Tomos or Seren I will hold you responsible. And I will seek you out. Because

I am experienced in these matters also, my father and my father's father both being *dynion hysbys* and men of craft. So beware, Sir.'

The Crow nodded. For a moment Seren thought he would say something mocking but when it spoke its voice was quiet. 'I undertake to guard them with all my power.'

'That is all I ask.' Denzil stepped back. He glanced at Gwyn. 'We'll guard the Plas. This day is Midsummer and the longest day. A time of magic and music. A dangerous day. Come on, boy.'

Gwyn nodded. He whispered to Seren, 'Take care.'

'We will! See you later. At the Ball.'

Then they were out of the iron-hung gate and running across the lawn.

'Which way?'

'West,' the Crow snapped. 'Through the wood.'

9

A red boat

In the world of song and flight
Birds decide what's wrong or right.

Seren was a little worried, remembering her encounter with Them among the trees, but this time the wood was empty and softly lit with golden afternoon light. They ran through glades of oak and under the great smooth boughs of beech, where the ground was bare underneath.

Beyond the wood was a gate in the wall. Beyond this, to left and right, a cart track ran between the fields. The Crow flapped left.

It was still very warm. Soon the Crow got tired. 'I'll have to ride on your shoulder, Seren. Or else my clockwork will run down.'

Seren nodded. As he flew down and settled himself, she looked up and saw that the whole of the sky in front of them was red, and that the track led down to a small river, running between willows.

'Down there?' Tomos said. 'That's the stream.'

'Quite right,' the Crow muttered.

'So you do know the way?'

The Crow shrugged. 'The other world is always very close. Turn a corner, cross a field, and you find it. You just have to want to. West is always a good way to start.'

The stream was clear. Weed streamed green along its shallow bed.

They scrambled down the bank and Seren said, 'Yes, look. There!'

Two boats were tied alongside the bank. One was blue and one was painted red like a child's toy, and each had two oars folded neatly in the bottom.

'Blue,' Tomos said at once.

'Red,' the Crow commanded.

They climbed in. 'I want to row!' Tomos and Seren said at the same time.

Seren grinned. She took an oar and Tomos took the other and they pushed the red boat away into the small stream and started to row. She had never done it before. It wasn't at all easy. She kept missing the water altogether and splashing herself, and Tomos was no better. They giggled and the Crow got cross.

'Why are you even bothering?' it said. 'The stream is taking us along quite fast enough.'

That was true. At first the water had flowed gently between the banks, but now Seren realised that it was faster and a lot deeper. Also, the trees on each side were closing in, so that the river ran through a green tunnel of branches.

A kingfisher watched them pass underneath its branch.

'Is this right? How far do we have to go?'

'Until we get there.' Now that they had started the Crow seemed to be more uneasy. He perched on the stern and kept looking back over his shoulder.

'What's wrong?' Seren asked.

She frowned and looked back too. The stream had twisted so she couldn't see far, but she thought she heard, a long way behind, the swish of oars. 'Do you think some of Them have got in that other boat?'

'Maybe. We should have sunk it,' the Crow muttered. 'Why didn't you think of that!' He turned to face the front, and stared.

Ahead of them was no stream now but a full-sized river, and they were being swept along faster than they could row.

Suddenly the roar of the water was noisier.

Tomos called out something that sounded like, 'Rooks!'

'No time for birdwatching,' the Crow said.

Tomos yelled again, and pointed. 'There!'

Seren peered closer. 'Not rooks,' she murmured. 'I think he means...'

'ROCKS!' Tomos screamed.

The boat slewed. Seren gave a cry. Everything was wrong; they were bumping up and down, flung sideways. She dropped her oar and it fell into the water; she grabbed over the side for it but it was already gone.

Tomos pulled her back.

The Crow was hunched down, wet and miserable. 'Lord, how I hate adventures,' he muttered.

Now the boat was quite out of control. They had to hold on tight as it whirled and sped past high banks hollowed with holes, under trees, out into deeper currents.

'What can we do?' Seren yelled.

'Where's the Egg?' Tomos rummaged for it.

'No! Don't get it out! We'll lose it. And…' She stopped. Suddenly she could hear a deep, thundering roar. It came from ahead, round a bend in the river, and it was getting louder all the time. 'Oh no,' she whispered.

The boat almost tipped over. It rounded the bend and the noise redoubled.

'It's a *waterfall*!' Tomos yelled. He looked at her. 'Seren. Can you swim?'

'Not a stroke,' she whispered.

'Neither can I,' the Crow wailed.

The roar of the water was terrible. As the boat swirled closer to the falls they were deafened with it. Seren could barely hear what Tomos was shouting.

'Jump! I'll … you … safe…'

'No!' she yelled. 'I can't!'

She had never been so scared. And she was soaked, her hair plastered to her face.

The Crow was huddled in the bottom of the boat. 'Fly away,' she yelled at it. 'Before we go over!'

The falls must be very close but there was nothing to see but spray and rainbows. The Crow took no notice of her. It was muttering something. It had its head in Tomos's bag; it was talking but she couldn't hear a word it was saying.

Then it re-emerged, dragging something round and silvery.

The mirror?

It was too heavy. The Crow dropped it, hopped up and yelled in her ear.

'Throw it overboard!'

What?'

'THROW IT OVERBOARD!'

For a second she just stared. Then, taking a breath, she knelt up in the swirling boat, picked up the mirror and threw it. It went flashing through the air, and landed with a great splash between two sharp rocks.

It sank at once.

'What use was that?' Tomos yelled.

Seren shook her head.

But wait!

Something was happening. Where the mirror had slashed into the water, a circle of ripples was beginning. It grew smoother and wider. She saw that the whole river was slowing and growing and changing, that it was transforming even as she watched, all the rocks submerging, all the splash and bubble smoothing out.

The waterfall's roar slowed to a gurgle, then a sluggish splash, then nothing.

The boat was floating in the middle of a wide silver lagoon.

'Gosh,' Tomos said.

Seren was so breathless she couldn't say anything. Instead she pushed wet hair out of her eyes and stared all round.

The water was serene. Silvery moonlight glittered on it. Dark woods surrounded it and beyond them the sky was purple.

A sniff from beside her. The Crow preened its feathers smugly.

'That is amazing!' Seren grabbed the Crow and kissed it on top of its head. 'You saved our lives!'

The Crow spluttered and squawked. 'Get off, you silly girl. Some of us come prepared for these things, that's all. It's always just as well to have a few useful items around. Of course, I make it a point to look forward and back. I...' He stopped and narrowed his jewel-bright eyes.

Following his gaze, Seren saw, far away and as small as a pin, the blue boat. Someone was in it, but they were hopelessly far away.

'And that's sorted Them too!' the Crow said with satisfaction.

'Well, can you magic up some oars?' Tomos asked. 'Because we've lost ours and we're not going anywhere.'

That was true.

The boat was completely still.

'Hmmm,' the Crow said. 'Kek kek.'

Seren shivered.

It was quiet and creepy. The water was so wide she couldn't see any banks, just a faint mist rising around them. But then she realised the boat had begun to move. Very silently and softly a deep current was taking them towards the setting sun.

'We're going somewhere now,' the Crow said darkly. 'Better sit back and enjoy it.'

Seren was only too glad to squeeze the water out of her clothes and push the hair from her face. Tomos checked his bag, then pulled out the Box. He peeped in at the Egg.

'Is it all right?'

'I think so. A bit bumped about.'

The Crow groaned. 'For Heaven's sake, keep it safe in case she turns me into something else. There are worse things than being a Crow. A Clockwork Spider doesn't bear thinking about.'

The boat drifted silently and slowly. Seren sat in the prow and Tomos on the little bench for the oarsman. Neither of them spoke, and for a moment she fell into a daydream. It was so sleepy here. And the sun should have been setting, but it hung in the purple sky, as if Time had slowed right down, or didn't exist at all.

Then, with a bump that startled Seren wide awake, the boat hit the shore.

Quickly, she jumped out.

Her boots sank into wet shingle.

She looked round.

They were in a dense forest of oaks. It looked dark and still.

'Pull the boat right up,' the Crow commanded. 'And then carry me ashore. I don't want to get my feet wet and catch a cold.'

Tomos sighed. He jumped out and helped Seren; they couldn't drag the boat very far into the trees but it was enough. Then Seren picked up the Crow. His wiry talons dug painfully into her fingers.

'Careful now. Put me on that log.'

She let him hop down.

He looked around in disgust. 'Well, I haven't a clue where we are. This journey is not turning out as it should. We might be miles from the Swan's Garden.'

Seren said, 'I think…'

But that was all she had time for. Because at that moment a rickety cage fell from the tree overhead and neatly captured the Crow. He gave a great squawk and fluttered against its wooden bars. 'What the… Get me out of here! NOW!'

Seren tried to spring up but to her astonishment she was caught too. A soft mesh, delicate as cobweb had come down all over her and Tomos, trapping her arms and tangling round her legs. The more she struggled with it the worse it got.

'Let me out!' she yelled, and Tomos was shouting, too, but the Crow had gone strangely silent.

At last, breathless, she stopped and looked at him.

He was staring upwards. Seren followed his gaze.

The trees were not empty.

Three owls sat there.

Two were ordinary brown owls but the central one was a huge, snow-white creature with amber eyes.

The Crow drew himself up. 'What is the meaning of this ATROCITY? I DEMAND TO KNOW...'

'You're under arrest,' the white owl said. Its voice was soft and sinister.

'Arrest?' The Crow was astonished. 'What for?'

'Illegally impersonating a bird.'

'But...'

'Save your defence for the court.' The owl swivelled its head right round. 'Take them,' it said.

With a flutter of feathers four huge eagles swooped down from the trees. One took the cage and the other three snatched up the corners of the net. Seren gave a gasp, because suddenly she was in the air, tumbled together with Tomos, being carried high above the trees.

'What's going on?' he muttered in her ear.

'I don't know. Just hold on to the Box and the other things. Keep your ears open and your eyes on me.'

'But if he's been arrested...!'

Seren sighed. 'It's ridiculous. For being a bird! He'd hardly fool anyone. He's more moth-eaten than ever.'

They flew so high over the trees that cloud drifted around them, then just as quickly they were descending and, as the eagles circled, Seren wriggled round so that she was lying on her stomach and could see where they were going.

'Tomos' she gasped. '*Look!*'

Below them was a vast ruin.

It might have once been a castle, now it was a mass of black walls and ivy-covered towers.

Roofless turrets rose against the sunset.

And everywhere there were rustles and flutters and chirps.

'It's full of *birds*!' she whispered.

There were thousands of them! As the eagles flew down Seren saw that the bigger birds were perched high on the walls; buzzards, hawks, guillemots, storks and egrets, white in the moonlight. Below them were ranks and ranks of smaller ones. There were tits and finches, starlings and sparrows, robins and wrens and many more she couldn't even recognise.

As she landed with a bump and rolled out of the net, their million eyes watched her.

She sat up in a vast arena of fluttering and preening.

Swallows and swifts, too nervous to perch, flitted through the twilight. Ducks and geese and ptarmigan sat comfortably on the ground. A peacock spread its gorgeous tail with a rustle. Hummingbirds darted like bright flies.

Seren put her hand down on the forest floor and then pulled it away quickly. 'OH!'

All the ground was rough with pellets. They were made of tiny clots of crushed bones, teeth and skulls.

'Yuk,' Tomos said.

The three owls flew down and landed heavily. The huge Snowy Owl blinked its amber eyes. They were round as coins and fixed on her.

The small cage was delivered by the fourth eagle, and then it was lifted away and the Crow sat there.

It stared out at the parliament of birds.

'Good heavens,' it muttered.

But the Eagle Owl was speaking. 'You! What is your name?'

The Crow cleared its throat. 'First of all I demand to know under what authority we have been brought here. I *demand* to know how...'

'Answer the question!' The eagle came back and landed beside him. It had an extremely sharp beak.

The Crow was still a moment. Then it snapped, 'My name is Mordecai Marchmain.'

'What are you?'

'I'm sorry...?'

'What species?'

'Human, of course.'

A whisper of astonishment and disgust went through the ranks of birds.

'Then why,' the owl asked severely, 'are you falsely wearing the skin and feathers of our brothers? The Corvid family, to be exact.'

It flicked a wing to the left. Seren saw that part of the ruin was black with rooks and crows and ravens and jackdaws and choughs, all of them looking extremely angry.

She didn't like this at all.

'They are the ones who have brought this prosecution,' the owl went on smoothly. 'And you should be warned that it is a capital charge. You will have a chance to speak for yourself shortly. First, however, the prosecution will call its witnesses.'

The Crow was so astonished it was speechless.

The witnesses were more than ready.

A whole row of starlings whistled eagerly together. 'We saw this being fly through the sky on wings. Lots of times. Even down a chimney.'

A swallow said sweetly, 'I certainly heard this being say *kek kek.*'

A robin hopped forward. 'I saw this being on very many occasions peck, preen and flutter. Not very expertly, though, I have to say and his feathers are a disgrace.'

A small wren with a very big voice announced, 'I saw this creature hop on the lawn.'

A dove cooed, 'I saw this creature scratch itself with its talons.'

The owl nodded. 'Thank you all. This is very damning evidence. He is clearly pretending to be a bird, though I agree it is a very tatty plumage and an insult to the avian species.'

'This is totally ridiculous,' the Crow snapped.

'Remove your disguise,' the owl said.

'I can't.'

'Why not?'

'Because it was put on me by a spell.' The Crow's voice was acid. Its jewel-bright eye glinted. 'I am actually on my way right now to get the spell removed and yet you have the nerve to bring me here by force and...'

'Do you mean,' one of the other owls asked curiously, 'that you don't actually want to be a bird?'

The Crow looked as though it would explode with wrath. 'Good grief...! *Why on earth would I WANT to be a bird!* It's a nightmare! All that pecking and hopping and not being able to pick things up properly! I can't write! I can't sit down and I can't stand up. I haven't had a proper bath for years. I have absolutely nothing to eat, not even worms. Goodness! A worm would be a banquet! My feathers are moth-eaten and my talons are made of wire. I HATE being a bird.'

There was a huge sensation of fluttering and whispering. If the birds had been cross before they were really angry now.

Seren glanced at Tomos. 'He's just making things worse.'

'He usually does.'

'And anyway,' the Crow folded its wings and yelled above the uproar, 'all the scientists tell us that birds have very little intelligence and I have PLENTY.'

Seren had never heard such an uproar.

'We have to do something,' Tomos hissed, 'or they'll peck him to bits!'

Seren nodded.

She stood up. 'Excuse me,' she said.

The uproar continued.

'EXCUSE ME!'

The Snowy Owl blinked at her. Then it held up a wing.

Slowly the noise died down. All the birds stared at Seren.

'Is that a chick?' someone asked.

The owl glared at the Crow. 'Is that one of your chicks?'

'Dear me, no.' The Crow frowned at her. 'I just look after it. Her.'

'It's someone else's, then? A cuckoo's?' All the birds turned and glared resentfully at a large brown bird on a branch all by itself. The cuckoo shrugged.

'I can talk, you know,' Seren said. 'Look, you've called witnesses against him, so it's only right that he can call some on his side. So I'm a witness. And I can tell you that he isn't a real bird or even pretending to be, so…'

'Have you *actually* seen him in human form?' a magpie snapped.

'Well … no, but…'

'He's just told you some story then. Is he usually truthful?'

Seren squirmed. 'Well … no … that is…' She caught the Crow's eye. 'But you can clearly see he isn't real. He's all moth-eaten. And there's that key. Sticking out of his back. Do you see it?'

All the birds nodded.

'Well, that winds him up. And if it isn't wound he runs out of clockwork.' She winked at the Crow. 'He sort of *goes to sleep*.'

The Crow was staring at her.

She winked again, urgently. 'It's happening now. See?'

Suddenly the Crow understood. It closed its eyes, and its movements got slower and slower until it was perfectly still. Then it fell over and lay on the ground.

One of the jackdaws hopped down and walked all round it, eyeing it curiously. 'Is it dead?'

'No, it will come back if I wind it up.' Seren held out her hands. 'So that's not like a normal bird, is it? A real bird?'

The birds murmured doubtfully.

She took a step nearer the Crow.

The ancient owl hooted for silence. It drew itself up.

'I'm afraid your argument is not at all convincing. You don't really know if he is human. You say yourself that he tells lies. And all birds sleep, then wake up again.'

'But…' Seren said.

'We've heard quite enough. It's time to take a vote. All in favour of innocent?'

Not a feather moved.

'All in favour of guilty?'

Every wing rose with a rustle.

Seren's eyes went wide. 'Wait! But you can't…!'

The owl's voice was not so soft now. 'The verdict of the court has been given,' it said mercilessly. 'Humans are not allowed to pretend to be birds and an example has to be made. This miserable creature will be taken to a secret place and pecked apart, and may…'

'You can't! It's not his fault!' Seren had lost her

temper now, she shouted the words as loud as she could. 'Anyway, the spell was put on him by a bird!'

'Nonsense,' the owl snapped. 'What bird could possibly...'

Seren took a breath. 'As a matter of fact,' she announced, 'it was *the Midnight Swan*!'

10

Down the well

Let the moonlight in your heart.
Where the secret journeys start.

There was utter silence.

The Crow opened one eye.

All the birds sat rigid, as if they dared not move.

Then the very smallest, a firecrest, piped up in a tiny voice 'Did she say…?'

'*Shhhh,*' a thousand birds hissed at once.

And instantly, they all flew. It was deafening and terrifying, the lift-off of a million wings. Feathers and dust rained; bricks fell from the ruined towers. Seren and Tomos had to duck under the up-draught of that panicked flight, the gulls yelping and the jays screeching, all the tiny birds swirling together in terrified packs, the geese honking away in hurried V formations, the peacock stalking swiftly into the wood.

Finally, the screeching and scratching and slither faded out to a distant roar and swirl of wings high in the sky.

Silence came back.

A single feather floated slowly down.

The Crow uncurled from where it lay flat, wings over its head. 'Goodness.' It sat up, and brushed dust from itself, 'That was … er … quite an experience.'

Tomos was looking up into the sky. 'They were so scared! When you said about the Midnight Swan, they were all terrified.'

Seren nodded.

'It was a great plan!'

'Yes,' she said. Though, actually, that hadn't been the plan. She had been going to pretend she saw a cat coming through the wood. But maybe that wouldn't have scared them as much, she thought.

The Crow spat out dust. 'Well, it was lucky I thought of it, then. Things could have got quite nasty…'

'It wasn't you.' Tomos picked up his bag and checked the Box was secure. 'It was Seren. And you shouldn't keep trying to take the credit.'

The Crow waggled its head, annoyed. 'Yes. All right.'

Seren looked around. 'Come on. Let's go quickly in case they come back. Towards the sunset is this way.'

There was a narrow path heading west and she hurried along it, Then, because she was so worried about the time, she ran. They had to deliver the Egg and get back for the Midsummer Ball, because the Tylwyth Teg would be there and who knew what might happen! She had visions of coming back and finding a hundred years had passed! Plas-y-Fran would be a ruin, all its roofs gone and the gables standing stark against the sky. Rain would be falling on the carpet of the grand staircase. Or maybe it would all just be magicked away like the palace in Al-Adin, far away across the sea, with Captain Jones and Lady Mair and Denzil and Sam the cat and everyone else inside it.

She looked up.

The sun had set.

The sky was darker, and the first stars were coming out.

The path had narrowed; now it ran between high hedges. Swooping in front, the Crow landed awkwardly. Then it looked back, its head cocked.

'What?' Seren gasped, catching up and holding her side.

'*Ssssh*!' The Crow listened intently. Then it frowned. 'Someone is still following us.'

Seren couldn't hear a thing. 'Are you sure?'

'Totally. I can hear footsteps. Steady and swift.'

'Who can it be?' Tomos came close; for a moment they all listened until Seren thought she could hear something too.

'Is it Them? From the other boat?' she whispered.

'Who else could it be? They want that Egg back. They want me to stay a bird for ever.' The Crow scowled. 'Well, that's never going to happen. At once, please, Tomos. The pin-cushion!'

Now Seren could definitely hear something walking soft and stealthy through the dark. 'Quick!' she hissed. 'Hurry up!'

Tomos had the pin-cushion out. He turned his back and threw it over his shoulder, at the very same moment that a tall, dark figure turned the corner.

Instantly a thicket of thorns filled the lane.

It was so high it couldn't be climbed, and so thick and tangled it couldn't be seen through. Black sharp thorns, spiny as pins, big as corkscrews, sprouted out everywhere.

'HA! Let Them get through THAT!' the Crow smirked. It dusted its wings together with satisfaction and turned. 'Let's go.'

Seren turned too. Then she stopped. A faint muffled shout of dismay had come from the other side of the thorn thicket. For a moment she hesitated. It didn't actually sound like Them. But then she remembered that They were full of all sorts of tricks. You could never be too careful.

She ran after Tomos and the Crow.

The path led them down into a dry ditch and then up and up onto a grassy hill. Now they were running on open turf under a sky that was definitely full of stars, and far off in the east the moon was rising: a silver globe.

Against it, on the very top of the hill, something dark was sitting.

Tomos slowed, cautious. 'What's that?'

The Crow scrambled up onto Seren's shoulder and stared. 'Not sure. Better go carefully.'

They climbed the rounded hill. At the top was a barrow, humped against the sky, and sitting on top of the barrow, watching them come, was a hare.

The hare was brown. Its long ears lay flat to its head. Its legs were powerful and built for speed. But what fascinated Seren were its eyes, huge and round and positioned on each side of its head as if it could see all around itself, even behind.

As if it could see the past and the future.

The silver moon reflected in its stare, the hare watched them come.

When they got close, Seren stopped. 'Hello,' she said.

The hare was silent.

'Maybe you can help us. We're looking for a garden. And we're in a bit of a hurry.'

The hare just stared.

'It's the garden of the Midnight Swan,' Seren said. She hadn't been sure about saying that. She thought the hare might just bolt in panic, like the birds had done. But it didn't move, except for the slightest twitch of one ear.

'Come on.' The Crow turned away in disgust. 'This is just a stupid creature that doesn't…'

'Down the well,' the hare said.

Seren shivered. Its voice was harsh and silvery. It made her feel cold just to listen to it.

'I'm sorry? Did you say down the…?'

'Well.' The hare was so still it was just a silhouette against the moon.

'Thank you,' Seren said, not knowing what else to say.

'Also…'

'Yes?'

'Beware.'

'Beware? Beware of what?'

'Everything.'

Tomos whispered, 'He doesn't say much, does he?'

Seren nodded. 'Thank you,' she said again.

'Pleasure.' The hare remained staring at them.

But the Crow wasn't satisfied. 'You're not actually being very helpful. *Everything*? And how can a garden be down a well? It's hardly likely. It could all be some kind of trap.'

The hare didn't even blink.

'Please yourself,' it said. Then it raised its head and stared at the moon.

'Is it far, this well?' The Crow demanded.

But the hare didn't answer at all. And when Seren looked into its eyes she saw they were filled with the silver glory of the moon, and for a moment all she wanted to do was stay there, too, and stare and stare at the alien, cratered surface, so that its brilliant light filled all her eyes and her head and her brain and…

'*Seren*!' Tomos whispered.

She blinked.

The Crow was already stalking down the other side of the hill in disgust.

'Don't just stand there. Come on.'

Seren followed but she couldn't help looking back. The hare had not moved. And if it could see into the future…

'Are they going to send me away?' she whispered.

The hare's eyes were pools of moonlight. For a moment she thought it hadn't heard her, but then it said softly, '*There is no such place as away*.'

She didn't know what that meant, but it was strangely comforting. She was scared to ask any more, and turned and hurried after Tomos and the Crow. All the way down the dark slope the grass was soft and springy under her feet, and tiny pale flowers studded the hillside, and at the bottom, just as the hare had said, was the well.

Seren and Tomos approached it cautiously.

It stood alone in the empty grass, an ancient, mossy circular wall, with a few moths and damselflies flitting above it.

They leaned over and looked down.

It was utterly black, and there was an eerie drip, drip, drip from far down in the depths.

'We have to go down there?' Tomos wondered. 'Yuk.'

The well took his words and whispered them back at him, round and round and down and down, *yuk yuk yuk yuk yuk,* until it seemed that there were a hundred voices clustered at the bottom, all murmuring back.

Seren shrugged. She didn't like the look of it either. But she climbed up on the wall and swung her legs over.

'Be careful, girl!' the Crow snapped.

'There's a ladder down the inside.'

Her feet found the top rung and then the next, and she put her weight on them slowly. They looked like rusty old iron but they seemed strong enough. Seren twisted round and started to climb down.

After a few rungs she said, 'It's wet and horrible. And dark.'

Her own voice sounded strange and hollow.

'Wait for me.' The Crow fluttered down and onto her shoulder.

Seren rubbed her forehead with the back of her hand.

This looked scary.

As she climbed down everything got darker. The circle of sky above shrank and then, when Tomos swung himself over and started to climb down too, dust and dirt showered all over her. Her hands slipped on the wet powdery rust; her fingers were red with it.

She was out of breath.

'Interesting mosses,' the Crow remarked. '*Homalothecium Camptothecium sericeum* if I'm not mistaken.'

Seren gritted her teeth. His talons were gripping her shoulder so tight it hurt.

Down and down. The circular walls closed in. Drips soaked her face and clothes. The stink of stagnant water made her feel sick.

She was so tired she wanted to stop, but there was nowhere to stop so she just had to keep going. Just when she felt her arms were so stiff she couldn't hold on any more she noticed something.

It was getting lighter.

'Of course,' the Crow said in its lecturing voice, 'countries at the bottom of a well are not that unusual. In the Celtic and Germanic mythologies they happen all the time. They...'

'Be quiet,' Seren whispered. Because suddenly she was not climbing down, but up!

How had this happened?

She was still going the same way, but now that way was definitely up, and the light was above her, and the dark well below, and it was harder to drag her weight up and her arms ached.

It was so odd it made her dizzy to think about it.

But a silvery timeless light was around her now. She could smell flowers, a rich overpowering scent of roses and lavender. The Crow gave a *kek kek* of excitement. 'We're near the garden! I know it!'

Then Seren's face came out into the light. She gave a whoop and pulled herself over the lip of the well and collapsed into the grass.

Tomos fell next to her.

The Crow hopped off.

For a moment they all gasped and panted. Then Tomos stared. 'I don't understand. We're back where we started!'

'No.' The Crow looked around at the grassy hill and the moonlit sky. 'We're not quite. It's upside down. Inside out. Though I'm not sure which way is west.'

'*You'll have to follow me.*'

The Crow turned. 'What?'

'I didn't say anything.' Seren looked at Tomos. 'What do you mean, follow you?'

Tomos was checking the Box was safe in his satchel. He looked surprised. 'That wasn't me.'

'Well, it wasn't me,' Seren said.

'Nor me,' the Crow snapped.

'*It was me.*'

They all looked at each other.

Then they looked down.

Seren knelt, and parted the high grass.

'About time,' the tiny voice said crossly. 'I've been waiting here ages.'

11

Zigzag cracks

Lake and roses, tower and bell,
is it time to break the spell?

A small yellow mouse sat among the grass stalks.

'Hello,' Seren said. She had decided that it would be what she always said to talking beasts from now on.

'Good evening,' the mouse said, politely.

The Crow hopped nearer and inspected the mouse closely with its bright blue eye.

'Don't even think about it,' the mouse snapped.

'About what?'

'Eating me.'

'*Kek kek*,' the Crow said, annoyed. 'I can't stop

thinking about it, but unfortunately I'm totally unable to do it. Luckily for you.'

'Good.' The mouse's voice was as tiny as it was, but immensely self-assured. 'Of course, I'm under the protection of the Swan. So it would be a really bad idea. Well, there's no time to lose. But first, did you know you're being followed?'

'WHAT!' The Crow jumped up in its fury. 'STILL?'

Seren looked at Tomos. 'They got through that thicket?'

'Must have.'

'Someone is climbing up the well at this very moment.' The mouse flicked a self-important whisker. 'We need to move.'

It jumped up on Tomos's coat, ran down his sleeve and into his pocket. Its head popped out.

'All right. Let's go!'

Tomos grinned.

'Across the field that way,' the mouse ordered. 'And run!'

Tomos ran. Seren raced after him, the Crow flapping along behind. But before they had even reached the orchard on the far side of the field the mouse squeaked, '*Too late!*'

Seren looked back. A pair of long white hands had appeared over the top of the well.

'They've caught up,' she gasped. 'At least…'

The Crow screeched to a halt. 'This time I'll really sort Them out … Tomos, *the glass pyramid*.'

Tomos already had it in his hand.

Seren said, 'Isn't that…?'

'From the drawing-room cabinet, yes. I'll be in real trouble.' Tomos turned his back.

'Yes, but wait,' Seren said quickly. 'Before you throw it… It's just, I'm not sure it is Them, after all and…'

It was too late.

He had already tossed the small, crystal pyramid over his shoulder. It spun flashing through the starlight, tumbled onto the grass, and lay there.

'Magic?' the mouse asked.

'What else?' the Crow said haughtily.

For a moment Seren thought nothing was happening, but then a tall, thin man heaved himself out of the well and waved frantically. He shouted and jumped up and down. 'Brother! It's me! ENOCH!'

The Crow's beak opened; a small gasp came out.

Too late! The crystal pyramid burst open. It shot up and out, higher and higher until it was a glass mountain that blocked the sky, glaciers and peaks sparking upward, vast mountain fissures opening like chasms with terrible cracking sounds that made Seren and Tomos crouch down in fear.

Then, silence.

The glass mountain stood slippery and sheer. How could anyone climb that?

'Oh hell!' the Crow said softly.

'That was your brother! *He*'s the one who's been chasing after us all this time!' Tomos stood up and went and touched the nearest crystal edge with his hand. It felt icy cold. 'How on earth is he going to get over this?'

'Well, how was I supposed to know?' The Crow hunched huffily in the grass. 'How am I supposed to know EVERYTHING? You'd be more than happy with a mountain if it was Them behind us! Admit it!'

'Yes, I would, but...'

'Then stop blaming me.' The Crow turned away. 'Enoch will just have to do the best he can.'

'I think it was quite impressive,' the mouse remarked kindly.

The Crow nailed it with a wintry glare. 'Come on,' it snapped.

Seren frowned. She knew that the Crow was bitterly sorry not to have Enoch here. But he would never admit he'd been too hasty. That just wasn't how he was. Still, she caught up with him and whispered, 'I'm very sorry about Enoch.'

The Crow allowed himself a sigh. 'So am I. But he is very resourceful. He's learned a lot from me, of course.'

'Through the orchard,' the mouse ordered. It flicked a whisker. 'And do hurry, because She is waiting.'

The orchard was beautiful. Under the summer moon, its perfect fruits hung ripe – golden apples and silver pears – and the dark grass was studded with daisies.

At the end of the small trees they reached a great stone wall, and the Crow gave a shiver of excitement. 'This is it! Goodness, I remember it so well! This is the wall of the garden. There's a gate…'

'There it is,' the mouse said, pointing a minute paw over the top of Tomos's pocket. 'Just there.'

It was exactly how Seren had imagined it: an

iron gate in an arch in the wall. She put her hand out, cautiously, and unlatched it.

The gate creaked open, and they went in.

They were inside the Garden of the Midnight Swan.

Her first thought was how beautiful it was. There were flowers everywhere, many of them roses, white and red, shimmering in the moonlight. The fragrance of their petals was heavy and sultry.

Nothing moved down the winding paths.

No leaf stirred in the clipped box hedges.

Everything seemed deeply asleep.

She saw that among the rose bushes were striped poles, topped with figures of lions and unicorns and dragons, all holding crests and shields. They were probably very brightly painted but in the moonlight they seemed all shadow and silver, and Seren thought their eyes opened and watched her sleepily as she passed beneath them.

Above the trees loomed the dark parapets and towers of a mighty castle, and she so wanted to go and explore it, but the mouse squeaked, 'No, this way, please, and keep up,' in its bossy little voice, and they turned left round a corner of the path.

And they saw the lake.

Seren breathed in.

It was a vast silver expanse. Moonlight shimmered on its surface like a magic pathway to a land of dreams. All around, black trees, heavy with leaf, stood against the starry sky.

'This is it!' she breathed.

'Yes,' the Crow muttered. 'This is it.'

She glanced at him. He looked more hunched up and moth-eaten even than usual. He fussed and fidgeted and preened a feather.

'It's all right,' Seren said kindly. 'After all we're bringing what She wants.'

'Yes, but you never know with these faery creatures. As I am always having to tell you, you can't trust them an inch.'

'Don't be tetchy.'

'I'm not tetchy.'

Seren opened her mouth to answer when Tomos said, 'Listen!'

From the high towers of the castle a bell began to chime.

Twelve slow, heavy chimes.

It was midnight.

'Just in time,' the mouse breathed a sigh of

relief. 'Well, that's my job done.' It jumped out of Tomos's pocket onto a low branch of honeysuckle. 'Now, if you'll take my advice, you'll…'

'We have no need of your advice, thank you,' the Crow said loftily. 'I can take it from here.'

The mouse wrinkled its nose. It looked at Seren, 'Feel a bit sorry for you. Having to put up with him.'

She shrugged. 'I know. But we love him.'

The Crow looked astonished.

The mouse nodded. 'Good luck then.' And with a flicker of its tail it was gone, running along the branch into a tiny hole in the wall.

'What a nerve these creatures have.' The Crow turned to Tomos. 'Quickly. The Box. We have to make sure the Egg is all right.'

Tomos pulled it out. The silver bands and the writing on the casket shone in the moonlight; he opened it and looked in.

His face went white. 'It's cracked!'

'WHAT?'

'There's a crack. But how … I've been so careful…'

'Let me see!' The Crow flapped over and stared. Seren wriggled in next to Tomos and saw it was true. There was a tiny crack, thin as a hair, in the perfect white shell.

At the same time, the singing began.

It was so sweet. High and strange and sad, it seemed to come from all around them.

'It's the roses,' Tomos breathed in awe. 'The roses are singing.'

Seren clenched her fingers tight, because the sound was so wonderful. It was stranger than the music of the Tylwyth Teg, because it was made by petal and sepal, and its sound was the sound of raindrops and seeds that grow in darkness, and its words were secret and pure.

As if in answer, from the lake ripples began to lap against the grassy bank, as if something was swimming towards them out of the darkness.

The Swan was coming, and the Egg was broken!

'What can we do?' she whispered.

'Nothing.' The Crow looked devastated. It turned to face the lake. 'Nothing at all.'

The swans swam silently out of the darkness, and their reflections shimmered on the moonlit water.

There were six white ones in a line; their proud

necks dipped and their beaks were black and gold. They looked beautiful and her heart gave a little shiver at seeing them. Behind them, black even against the blackness of the trees, came the Midnight Swan.

Seren felt afraid.

She had never seen a swan so big, or so graceful. Around its neck hung a collar of diamonds, each jewel sparkling tiny rainbows of moonlight. The Swan's eyes were dark and its beak was gold. And its gaze on her was cold and curious.

The swans arrived at the shore and their line parted, so that the black Swan could swim close to the shore. She looked at them all carefully, especially at the Crow.

'Don't I know you?'

The Crow cringed. 'Yes, Majesty. I had the honour of meeting you here many years ago. When I … er … unfortunately…'

The Swan's voice was icy. 'I remember! You were the schoolmaster who stole my rose!'

'I was.'

'And you've found your way back here. Why?'

The Crow gulped. Then it drew itself up. 'Because…'

But the Swan had caught sight of the Box, which Tomos was holding tightly in both hands.

'*What is that*?'

It heaved itself out of the water and onto the bank, all its feathers dripping. This close it was terrifying; its beak hard and dangerous, its eyes flashes of temper. 'That Box has my name on it. Why? And who are these children you've brought here?'

The Crow seemed too scared to speak.

Seren stepped forward. She was scared, too, but determined not to show it. 'We came because he's our friend and because it's not fair that he should be trapped in a bird shape. And we brought you something that you asked for.'

The Swan's face turned to her, zooming closer on its long neck. 'You are a bold little creature.'

Seren nodded. 'A lot of people have said that. I don't mind any more. But anyway, this is for you. I'm afraid it's got just a little cracked, but that's not our fault. It's a very awkward thing to carry and Tomos was really, really careful.'

She nodded to Tomos, who came forward and laid the Box down on the dark grass.

All the other swans gathered close to watch.

The roses bent lower.

The honeysuckle murmured.

The Midnight Swan stepped closer. It read the words on the side of the casket. '**If you can open My closed lid Your heart's desire Inside is hid.** This is a strange box with strange words on it. Where did you get it?'

'I … er … bought it,' Seren said. 'For a penny on a stall. Anyway, its not the Box but what's in the Box that matters.'

She knelt down, and opened the lid.

The Egg gleamed white in the moonlight. It would have been perfect, but for the crack, which had definitely grown bigger, she thought, even in the last few minutes.

The other swans gave small cries of joy and amazement but the Midnight Swan was absolutely silent. For a moment she didn't move at all. Then, her long neck stretching out, she carefully touched the Egg with her beak.

It rolled out onto the grass.

The Swan stared at it so long Seren thought she was angry. But then she raised her head and Seren saw two glistening tears. They fell onto the collar and became two more diamonds.

'You did it,' she said to the Crow. 'You found it!'

The Crow tipped his head on one side. 'I did, yes.' He squirmed a little and glanced at Seren. 'Well, actually it was…'

'He was very brave,' Seren said quickly. 'Especially in the boat…'

But the Swan was not listening. She gave a pure clear cry of anguish and pain and love. She bent down close to the Egg and breathed on it, and the warm summer night seemed to become even hotter, and it seemed that everything in the Garden, even the stars, crowded a little closer to see what would happen.

Sudden cracks zigzagged the Egg's hard shell. It split with a sharp, hard snap; then small pieces fell away and there was a hole, tiny, with something soft and strange moving inside the membrane.

'It's *hatching*,' Tomos breathed.

Seren laughed. She looked at the Crow. His jewel eyes were fixed on the hole in the Egg. Already it was bigger and they could see the beak of the chick inside, nibbling, struggling.

'Come,' the Swan said quietly. 'Come, my Cygnet.'

The Egg fell apart.

Moonlight shone on the creature that unfurled from it: a stiff, wet, weak creature, all awkward neck and gawky feet.

But it was clearly a cygnet, its downy fluff grey-white, its eyes blinking open.

All the garden gave a ripple of delight. The roses sang sweeter and the bells in the tower began to chime again but this time in glorious celebration. The cygnet tried to walk, fell over and tried again. It made a tiny squawk. At once the Swan gathered it into her flanks with her graceful neck, nuzzling it and comforting it.

When she looked up her eyes were bright. She looked full of joy, but her voice was still sharp.

'So, Master Crow. I have to admit that you have brought me my heart's desire. I suppose you want your reward now.'

The Crow was still staring at the cygnet with utter astonishment. He cleared his throat. 'Well … Yes … It would be very…'

But at that moment every face turned to look over his shoulder and all the swans hissed as one.

Seren turned quickly.

A bedraggled figure stood there.

He was tall and thin and his dark coat was torn

and his thin fair hair plastered to his skull. He was out of breath and his backpack hung empty and his walking stick was broken and there was a large bandage on his left big toe. But he looked triumphant.

'Mordecai,' he said, holding out both hands. 'It's me. I got here. I got here at last!'

12

Anything in all the world

Wish for love, wish for treasure
wish for someone else's pleasure.

The Swan bristled. 'Another thief in my garden? I'll turn this one into a toad this time!'

'No!' the Crow gasped, astonished. 'Don't do that! He's my brother, Enoch.' With a twitch of his wing he waved Enoch over.

The tall man came quickly over the grass. He nodded a little nervously at the Swan. 'I do beg your pardon, Ma'am … I don't mean to trespass. I've been following them all and trying to catch up but there were a few … er obstacles.'

'How on earth did you get through the thicket and over the mountain?' the Crow demanded.

'Well, I've learned a little magic, brother, after watching you over the years. I hope you don't mind. They were very good obstacles, though, I have to say. I've rarely seen better.'

The Crow looked a little less annoyed.

The Swan narrowed its eyes. 'Seeing as your friends have brought my son home I'll overlook your presence here. This once.'

'Much obliged.' Enoch nodded to Seren, 'Hello, Miss Seren. Very glad to see you.'

She bobbed a curtsey. 'And you.' It seemed a long time now since their first meeting in the railway waiting room, when he had given her the newspaper parcel, which contained the Crow.

'You've been a great friend to my dear brother, you really have. And you, too, Master Tomos.'

The Crow gave a splutter of irritation. He hopped closer to the Swan. 'Look this is all very well, and I'm delighted you have your cygnet back but, really, what about me? When are you going to take this spell off me? You promised and I really think it's time…'

The Swan hissed.

161

It seemed to swell and grow fiercer.

The Crow flapped hastily back.

'I made a promise and I will keep it,' the Swan said softly. 'But there is a difficulty. Are you certain – absolutely certain – that it was you who found my Egg?'

'Ah. Er … well …' The Crow threw a panicky look at Seren.

'Or…' the Swan swivelled its beautiful face to her, 'was it you?'

Seren was silent. She had no idea what to say. If she said the truth the Crow might never be human again.

'I um … well, the fact is…' the Crow's voice was strangled. 'It's not that straightforward…'

It was Tomos who spoke out. 'Seren got it,' he said suddenly. 'She just went out and found it, all by herself. It was really brave.'

The Swan nodded wisely. 'I suspected as much. So…' She turned fiercely to the Crow. 'The human girl found the Egg. The choice is hers.'

The narrow, black eyes, deep as night, regarded Seren. 'You have a choice now. Whatever you want, anything, in all the world, can be yours now. Just ask me for it.'

The Crow gasped.

Seren felt as if she was dizzy. *Anything in all the world!* She could ask for anything! There was so much she wanted. She could ask for Captain Jones to forget about sending her back to the orphanage! She could ask for Them not to be at the Midsummer Ball and for Tomos and Plas-y-Fran to be safe for ever! She could ask for a thousand books and to be a writer and as famous and clever as Mr Sherlock Holmes. She could even ask for gold and jewels and to be as beautiful as the dawn if she wanted, though to be honest she didn't care as much about those. Ideas went through her mind as swift as arrows.

They were all what she wanted.

She looked at the Crow.

The Crow looked back at her. He was completely silent. But she had never seen such a pleading in his jewel-bright eyes.

Seren sniffed. She tidied her hair and stood up straight. She felt as if what she was going to say next was the most important thing she would ever say in her life, and for a moment it scared her, because it would be final and she did really want those other things a lot. But when she spoke she made the words loud and clear. '*I want the Clockwork Crow to be back in his right shape again. If you please.*'

Enoch gave a great shout and Tomos clapped his hands and whooped.

The Crow gave a little explosion of relief and a few moth-eaten feathers burst upwards.

The Midnight Swan nodded its head. 'I see. Well, as you have asked for that, you'll have it. It was a generous act, because I can read in your heart that you have sorrows of your own. So, to show I can be generous too, I'll give you something for yourself. You will know how to use it when the time comes.'

'For me?' Seren whispered.

'Yes. Take this.'

The Swan lowered its neck so far that the collar of diamonds slipped off and fell on the grass.

'Oh!' Seren said.

She stared at the jewels, hardly daring to touch them.

'They'll solve one of your problems, I think,' the Swan said carelessly. 'But the human things I can do nothing about. Those are for you to solve.'

Seren knelt in the dark grass and picked up the

collar with both hands. It lay heavy on her palms, the diamonds glittering with cold brilliance, as if she held a constellation of stars. She was scared of how beautiful it was.

'Thank you,' she breathed.

'Er … ahem.' The Crow murmured hopefully.

The Swan turned its dark head. 'I haven't forgotten you. The child has asked for you to be unspelled, and I will tell you the way it must be done. But I warn you, it won't be easy.'

'You can't do it straight away?' Enoch asked, knitting his hands together. 'We've waited so long…'

'No. It is a fierce spell, spun in anger. A mighty enchantment. Such things cannot be undone with just a flick of a wing. There is a way but it will take courage. Especially,' she turned to the Crow, 'from you.'

The Crow looked anxious. 'I'll do anything.'

'Anything?'

'Anything.' But he sounded terrified.

'Then this is what has to be done.' The Swan fixed Seren with its dark gaze. 'You must take the Clockwork Crow apart, piece by piece. Every wheel, every cog, every feather. Beak and wings and claws. Then the pieces must be placed in a heap together under the full moon. *And they must be burned to ashes.'*

Enoch gasped.

Tomos said, 'Golly!'

Seren's eyes went wide. 'I can't!'

'You must. Because that is the only way the spell can be broken.'

The Crow looked dazed. 'I feel a little faint.'

'You must show your courage now.' The Swan rose gracefully and stretched its wings out, then it turned and slipped into the water with hardly a ripple, the cygnet snug in the downy feathers of its back, the tiny head gazing sleepily at Seren.

'But,' Seren hurried to the water's edge, 'what if we do all that and then … *it doesn't work*?'

'Trust me.' The Swan's voice came over the water, along the path of the moon. 'If you are brave, it will work. Goodbye now. Go through the silver gate, and good luck.'

The white swans followed her, a moonlit procession.

And the singing of the roses was a pure high note, until the swans vanished into the misty darkness, and only the moon was left.

The song of the flowers died away.

The garden was silent.

Seren turned. Her face was white. 'What are we going to do?'

No one dared answer.

Finally the Crow lifted its head with an effort and sat up. 'First we go back. Then … we do what she said.'

'Brother!' Enoch muttered.

'I have no choice.' The Crow shook itself irritably. 'Come on now, stop moping. Let's find this wretched gate and get out of here. I never want to see this place ever again.'

Enoch nodded sadly. He bent and picked the Crow up.

'It's over there.' Tomos had been looking about. 'See?'

The gate was a small silver one in the wall, and beyond it was a path that seemed to lead towards the castle. Seren led the way. As they hurried between the fragrant beds of roses and phlox and night-scented stock she wondered how on earth she would be able to do what the Swan had said.

It was impossible!

And a collar of diamonds! She could never

wear it; everyone would say it was stolen. What on earth was she to do with it? She clasped it tight round her waist, to keep it safe.

At the gate she stopped, breathless, the others crowding behind.

'Open it,' the Crow said. 'Quickly.'

The latch was silver. She pressed it down with her fingers and the gate opened and she walked through.

Onto the lawn of Plas-y-Fran.

Astonished, she heard the others come tumbling through behind her. In front of them the windows of the house were lit against the sky. The music of fiddles and harps was echoing across the lawn. Hundreds of lanterns hung from tree to tree.

'The Midsummer Ball!' Tomos breathed. 'But how...'

He glanced back.

The silver gate was still open; beyond it they could see the path, and the castle, deep in its fragrant garden. And then, slowly and silently the gate swung shut.

The night closed over it.

And it was gone.

'It's as if it was really just there all the time,' Enoch murmured after a moment.

'If we'd known that it would have saved us a world of trouble,' the Crow snapped. He turned. 'Someone's coming.'

It was Gwyn.

He ran out of the dark, breathless, 'Seren! Diolch byth, you're back! They are here and there and everywhere! Hundreds of them!'

'Where's Denzil?'

'They've got him! I don't know what to do!'

Seren scowled. 'Come on!' she yelled.

They fled across the lawn towards the jaunty lights. When they got to the gate she gasped because all the iron horseshoes and protective plants had been torn down and flung by spiteful hands all over the path.

Tomos pushed ahead of her. 'They are in my house, and it's my fault!'

He raced down the path.

'Silly boy.' The Crow sighed. 'After him, quickly!'

Tomos was already at the house. The door was wide open and light and music were streaming out. They saw him disappear inside.

'Wait, Tomos!' Seren yelled. She ran into the hall, up the stairs and burst through the wide doors of the ballroom.

She crashed into a dancer.

'Excuse me!' she gasped.

The dancer was tall and silver-haired.

'That's quite all right,' he said gravely, but as they waltzed away he laughed, and his partner, in a gold mask and dress, gave a mocking giggle.

Seren took a breath.

She looked down the long length of the room.

It was bewildering. In one corner the local musicians were playing, a harp and a fiddle and a crwth, but the music was all strange, and the musicians seemed sweaty and tired and baffled, as if they couldn't stop or even understand the sounds their instruments were making.

And the dancers!

Farmers and dairymaids, young girls from the village, local squires and their ladies, they whirled in a dream of strangeness, because among them and around them the Tylwyth Teg danced, too, tall and thin in their silver clothes, their hair glimmering, their eyes long, their mouths in wild laughter.

Could the mortals see Them?

Seren had no idea.

But surely they couldn't, because there was Denzil all tied up to a chair, and They were all around him, mocking and laughing and poking at him. His face was like thunder. Then he saw Tomos.

'No boy!' he snarled, 'Get out! GO!'

Tomos took no notice. He barged through the crowd with Seren after him. 'Leave him alone! Let him go!'

The Fair Family drew back. Amused, They let them through.

Tomos took out his penknife and tried to slash through the silvery bonds around Denzil's wrists and waist.

'That's no use,' the small man hissed.

'I'm going to get you free. I…' Then Tomos stopped. And turned.

Seren turned too. All around the strange tall silvery people were pressing close. Their masks were fox faces and swan eyes, they wore the ears of hares and the muzzles of wolves. Some were small and ugly. Some were winged like butterflies.

'*It's time, little Star,*' they whispered.

'*Time to come.*'

'*Time to join us.*'

'*As you promised.*'

'*Yes, you promised.*'

Tomos looked at Seren. 'What do they mean? You couldn't have promised to go with *Them*.'

'*Yes, she did.*'

'*Yes, she did.*'

'*In return for the Egg.*'

'*She did.*'

Behind her, the Crow groaned. 'Oh, you *silly* girl!'

13

A circle of friends

Rope of stars across the floor
Who could dare to ask for more?

Seren felt awful.

Tomos looked devastated and the Crow, who had flapped round and perched on the lamp, was glaring at her.

Beyond the circle of strange faces, the Ball was going on, but it seemed oddly distant.

Denzil struggled in his chair. 'You are not going with Them, Seren bach, be sure of that. Whatever happens…'

'But I made a promise, Denzil.'

'It should be me.' Tomos sounded bitterly unhappy. 'I brought the pen in.'

The Tylwyth Teg murmured. They put out their silvery fingers and touched his hair and sleeves.

'NO!' Seren pulled him away.

'*Then come, Seren.*'

'*Now, Seren.*'

'*The Moon is full.*'

'*The nights are shortest.*'

'*The roses are in bloom.*'

She felt so scared she was breathless. All her friends were here, but who could help her? She would have to be snatched away with the Fair Family, into their country of snow and strangeness, to that icy palace she had been in once before. And there was no time there, so she would live forever in a whirl of dancing and hunting and cold beauty, and there would be no one to talk to and no lessons and no books and no Sam the cat to play with and no Plas-y-Fran. Unless she visited it at night like a ghost, and watched everyone else growing older.

She shivered.

Above all, there would be no one to love her. But did she even have that now?

'I'm not having this!' Tomos folded his arms. 'If

they want a human child, they can have me. I'm not scared and I've been there before…'

'Close your mouth, you foolish infant!' the Crow snapped. It drew itself up. 'Clearly I am the one who should be sacrificed. All I have been is a source of trouble to my friends. I quite see that now. I will go and live in Their cage and amuse Them and…'

'No!' Enoch said earnestly. 'I haven't traipsed around the world for a hundred years trying to find a cure just for everything to fail now. I will go with Them and then you can all sort everything out without me and…'

'Nonsense!' Denzil snapped. 'This is *my* fight. I have warred against these beings for years. They will not have anything or anyone from Plas-y-Fran while I am alive. So if anyone has to go it will be me…'

'We need you here,' Gwyn gasped, scared but determined. 'I could take your place, Seren, if you like. I don't mind, really. You've always been very kind to me.'

Seren had tears in her eyes.

She sniffed them back.

This was no time to be silly.

'Thank you all,' she said, 'but I couldn't let any of you take my place.'

Which was all very well, but what on earth should she do? What would Mr Sherlock Holmes do? He would say, '*This is a very singular three-pipe problem, Watson,*' and then he would...

She stopped.

Problem.

That had been the word the Midnight Swan had used.

Suddenly an idea went right through her so fast it felt like a bright light. She drew herself up. She turned to face the sinister masks of the Fair Family.

'I made you a promise.'

'*Yes.*'

'I promised you I'd come if you want me to, were the exact words I said. But maybe I can offer you something else instead, something you'd like better than me.'

The Tylwyth Teg giggled and hissed. '*What else would interest us? What else would we want...*'

'My schoolmaster taught me about you.' Seren glanced at the Crow as she said it. 'There are two things you always hunger for. A human child is one. The other is ... treasure.'

At the same time she unbuckled the collar of diamonds from under her coat and laid it down on the shiny wooden floor of the ballroom.

The Tylwyth Teg gave a long, hissing gasp.

How the diamonds shone! They were like small facets cut from the face of the moon. They were the brightest thing in the whole brilliant room. They took light from everything and glinted it into rainbow shimmers that played over the narrow eyes and greedy hands of the clustering faery creatures. They were the tears of the Midnight Swan.

Seren said, 'You can have these instead of me. But you must go away and leave us all in peace from now on. No more trying to steal us away. No more trying to get into the house. Peace between us. For ever.'

'*Peace.*'

It was a whisper of awe.

'Yes. If you agree with all that you can have the diamonds.'

'You can't trust those creatures,' the Crow hissed in disgust. 'And what a waste of such a gift!'

She shrugged.

The Tylwyth Teg looked at each other. If they

spoke she didn't hear a word. But they must have a secret way of talking because they all nodded their heads one after another, all the beautiful, ugly, strange and sinister faces. Then one of them, a small dancer in a mouse-mask, bent and picked up the diamonds with a shiver of delight.

The shiver spread. It rippled through the crowd, through the mirrors, through the chandeliers. It rippled through the curtains and the floor. It rippled through Seren like the cold feeling you get when something delicious scares you.

The windows flew open. The music soared. And now all the dancers of the Fair Family were spinning and turning and laughing, and Seren was spinning with them till her head was dizzy and she was quite lost and sure they would snatch her away anyway. But at the last minute she held onto the doorknob tight and stamped her foot angrily.

'*There is no such place as away*,' she said.

Instantly, everything was changed.

She blinked.

The ballroom was just their ordinary drawing

room, with the furniture all taken out. The gauzy curtains drifted in a warm summer breeze. The dancers were the local village people in their Sunday clothes and they were all stopping, breathless, as if the dance had gone on too long. The musicians stopped playing with huge relief. They looked around as if something had happened and they had missed it.

And Lady Mair and Captain Jones were standing at the fireplace, smiling happily.

Lady Mair clapped her hands. 'Supper is served!' she said. 'In the next room. And then we will have a very special announcement!'

A murmur. All the farmers and their wives hurried out.

Someone grabbed Seren's hand; turning, she saw it was Mrs Villiers.

'Goodness, Seren, where have you been and why aren't you wearing your party dress? And you, Master Tomos, your face is quite smudged with dirt! Go and smarten yourselves up the pair of you. And Denzil! Why are you in here? Surely the guests' horses and carriages need...'

'Just going to see to it, ma'am.' Denzil was already out of the chair. He looked at Seren.

'Going, at once, now that everything is good here in the Plas.'

She smiled back at him, but she didn't feel that happy.

As he went out and Mrs Villiers turned away, she slipped after him.

'Denzil,' she said softly.

'What, Seren?'

But all of a sudden she couldn't answer. It was the Crow who said, 'We need a bonfire.'

14

Cinders and ash

Through the sadness, through the fire,
we will find our hearts desire.

In her room she put on a new midnight blue dress that Mrs Roberts from the village had made, and the little bracelet Tomos had once given her of berries and an acorn. She felt as if she needed all her special, magic things at a time like this. Looking at herself in the mirror she said firmly, 'Whatever happens, if the Crow is human again it will be worth it.'

Then she gave herself a determined nod, slipped out and ran downstairs, through the party room, onto the terrace and down the steps.

'Seren!' The whisper was Gwyn's. He was peering round the lilac bush. 'Over here.'

She ran over and went round the bush.

'It's in the stable yard,' he said. 'But why do you need a bonfire?'

Seren shook her head. 'You'll see.'

She could see the flicker of the flames even before she turned the corner of the stables. Denzil had lit it in an out of the way corner, by the wall, so as not to scare the horses.

It was small and bright and the wood blazed in the iron brazier.

Tomos was already there. Enoch was standing with his hands knotted together, more nervous than ever.

Only the Crow looked bold.

He was standing with his head held high and when Seren came closer he held out his wing and shook her hand with formal stiffness. 'Goodbye, Seren.'

'Don't say that!'

'Well, not for ever, of course. Just a few minutes really. But I just wanted to say … in case, well, these faery creatures, you can never quite trust them, so … I just wanted to say thank you.'

'What for?' she whispered.

'Well, lots of things … I mean, you are not perfect: you are stubborn, ridiculously fond of rubbish stories and have no idea at all how to behave like a young lady. But your Latin is coming on, your Maths is reasonable, and you do write an interesting paragraph. You have been a pleasure to teach. And er, ahem, of course, you have been a very good and loyal friend.'

Seren's eyes were wet.

The Crow coughed and harrumphed and suddenly flicked the key out of its side.

'Well then, let's get on with it. No point in hanging about. I'm sure it won't hurt a bit.'

Seren ran forward. She kissed the Crow on its moth-eaten head. 'You've never been a coward,' she said. 'And now you're really brave.'

The Crow looked a little surprised. 'Yes,' he said, 'I am rather, aren't I? Well, I have to saay thaaat I raaather hope I caaaannn keeeeppp it uppppppp….'

And then he was perfectly still, because the clockwork had run down.

Seren sighed.

'Let me help you', Enoch said anxiously. 'I know how to…'

'No.' She shook her head. 'It's all right, really. I can do it by myself.'

She took the Crow apart. It was just the opposite of when she had put him together, tugging off the wings and beak, unscrewing the cogs and wheels, unclicking the wiry talons. It was horrible but she tried not even to think about it, and in a few minutes a pile of pieces lay on the cobbles of the yard, with straw between the two jewel-bright eyes.

Tomos breathed out. 'That's so strange! I mean it's just bits now. So where is *he*?'

Seren shook her head.

Behind them, the music started up again.

Denzil looked at her. Then he said, 'I will do this part, bach, and don't say I won't.'

He picked up the pieces of the Crow, and very gently stacked them on the small fire.

They burned with a strange blue flame, and then a red crackle.

Seren pressed her lips together tight. She felt a touch on her fingers and Tomos's hand crept into hers. They stood and watched the fire burn, and Enoch stood next to them, quivering with nerves, his face as white as paper. Soon all the pieces of the Crow were nothing but ashes and twisted wire, and then they were gone altogether, falling down into the heart of the blaze.

They waited.

Nothing happened.

Over the lake, the moon laid a silver pathway. The midsummer stars wheeled across the sky. Bats flitted. The summer garden was a soft peace of sleeping flowers.

Inside the Plas, the harp was playing a gentle Welsh folksong.

Five minutes passed.

Ten.

Twelve.

'Where is he?' Seren whispered at last.

'Wait,' Denzil growled.

'But it's taking so long!' A terrible doubt was creeping into her mind and she couldn't stop it. What if it had all been a trap, a bitter revenge taken by the Swan? What if the Crow was gone and would never come back? What if…

'Seren!'

She turned.

Lady Mair was standing there with a lantern. 'Seren! Tomos! Come quickly!'

'But…'

'Come at once!' Lady Mair waved her hand. 'I need you here now!'

Seren looked at Denzil. 'Go,' he said. 'We'll wait here. See what happens. Go now.'

She couldn't move. *He thinks nothing will happen*, she thought, but then Tomos was pulling her with him towards his mother. Seren ran, too, but inside her was a horrible darkness, a deep grief that she thought she might fall into forever.

Lady Mair said, 'Oh, I've been looking for you everywhere! Come quickly!'

She caught Seren's hand and between the two of them she was pulled into the house.

Plas-y-Fran was open to the summer night, all its windows wide, all its doors ajar. They ran through the lavender-scented hall and up the stairs, and the lamps were bright and moths danced duets under the painted faces of the Jones' family, all of whom seemed to be smiling down at her in delight, their gilt frames gleaming.

Up, past dozens of guests, past Lily and all the maids clustered on the landing, past Mrs Villiers who touched Seren's arm and whispered, 'I'm so glad, dear,' and touched a tear from her eye with a handkerchief.

Bewildered, Seren said, 'What's happening? What's going on?'

'You'll see,' Tomos grinned.

Her heart beat fast. Her palms were hot. She was scared.

Past all the farmers and squires and ladies in the hot room, who squeezed aside and whispered.

Up to where Captain Jones stood, tall and waiting on the polished dais with the musicians, his tweed suit immaculate, his collar white as snow, his moustaches perfect.

'Seren,' he said. He held out a hand. 'Come up here, my dear.'

Breathless, she gasped, 'What's wrong?'

He smiled, and turned her round to face the crowd. 'Ladies and Gentlemen. All our dear friends. Thank you for stopping your merriment for just a moment. I have a very important announcement to make about my young friend here, Miss Seren Rhys.'

Baffled, Seren stared. Was this it? Was this when he would send her back to the orphanage? But why all the fuss and why all the people? And why was Lady Mair weeping and clutching Tomos's hand so hard it was red?

'You see,' Captain Jones went on, 'Lady Mair and I have become so fond of Seren that we have decided something momentous. Something wonderful. But first I would like to say how Seren has changed all our lives.'

A stir in the doorway.

Seren's eyes fixed on it. Someone came in and stood there.

'She has been such a joy. So happy, so generous, so clever, so sensible. She has lit up our home.'

It was a tall man in dark, shabby, very old-fashioned clothes. His face was lean and his nose was beaky. His eyes were jewel bright.

Seren gasped.

The lean man smiled. Behind him, out in the hall, Enoch was capering a silent jig.

'And so,' Captain Jones took her hand, 'we have made a great decision. All the legal work has been done. If she agrees, we are ready to adopt Seren into our family. She will be a real daughter to us, and a sister to Tomos. And from now on, her name will be Seren Rhys-Jones.'

He looked down at her and she stared up at him. 'Do you agree, Seren?'

Seren thought she could never get breath to answer. But she did, even though she could barely hear it herself.

'Yes. *Please*.'

Everyone laughed. Everyone applauded, loud and happy.

Captain Jones gave her a hug. Lady Mair ran up and flung her arms around her and held her close. 'I'm so glad, Seren!'

'So am I, Lady Mair.'

'No, no.' Lady Mair pulled back and looked at her with wet eyes. 'Mamma. You must call me Mamma now!'

Seren went quite still. Then she said, 'Thank you. Mamma.'

The Ball exploded into music and dancing. People kept coming up and shaking her hand and kissing her, the farmers' wives touching her hair and murmuring.

'Hyfryd.'

'Sweet thing.'

'So lovely!'

But Seren was too busy craning to see behind them, to see through the crowd. There was Denzil, sipping from a huge tankard of ale and raising a quiet hand to her, and there was Gwyn, eating the sandwiches hungrily.

And here was a tall, thin dark man in a shabby coat, who came up and bowed graciously.

'Is it you?' she gasped.

He straightened. 'Of course it's me. Who else would it be, you foolish girl.'

Seren thought she would faint from relief. She gave a loud whoop and everyone looked round and laughed.

'Oh, you should have seen it, Seren!' Enoch muttered. 'How there was smoke and chiming and song, and how he walked out of the fire not even singed.'

'Yes well, I'm here now.' He turned to Lady Mair and bowed. 'My name, Madam, is Mordecai Marchmain, Schoolmaster. At your service. I understand these children are without a tutor. Allow me to put myself forward. I have several degrees from various Oxford colleges in…'

He caught Seren's stern eye and stopped.

'Well. Maybe just one degree. But I assure you I am proficient in all subjects and will be perfect for your children. I already feel I know them very well.'

'It's very strange,' Lady Mair said, 'but I almost feel I know you, too. How wonderful!'

Mordecai Marchmain bowed gravely.

'Of course, you must come and teach them! But first, look! There are the fireworks!'

Loud cracks and bangs. Huge whoops and flashes of light. Everyone hurried outside. Tomos dragged his mother away and Captain Jones put his arms round a few friends and hurried them out.

Only Seren and the Crow were left.

'You know you'll always be the Crow to me,' she said.

Mordecai Marchmain shuddered. 'Good grief. I hope not. All those moth holes! All those itchy feathers. I will never forget it as long as I live.'

'Won't you miss it at all?'

'Not a bit. And if you'd been a bird for hundreds of years you wouldn't even ask so rubbish a question. *Kek kek.*'

Seren grinned. Suddenly she felt so happy she thought she would burst apart, so she ran towards the door. 'Come on! The fireworks!'

But his jewel-bright eyes had fixed on something. He hurried towards it. 'Just a moment.

Oh good heavens! Oh, how I have dreamed of this … I have craved … I can't tell you, Seren…'

A pile of creamy yellow cheese.

The Crow picked up a piece and nibbled it. 'Oh my goodness!'

He ate more. 'Oh heavens! Oh joy! Oh … fabulosity.'

Seren was dancing with impatience. 'Bring the plate with you,' she said, 'or we'll miss all the fireworks.'

But he was already piling plate on plate.

'I've got so much to catch up on. I'm as thin as a rake.'

Seren laughed. 'I don't think you will be for long,' she said.

And she dragged him outside, where the sky was a mass of falling golden stars.

The Clockwork Crow

Book one in the award-winning
Clockwork Crow trilogy

(Firefly Press, 2018)

When Seren Rhys is given a newspaper parcel by a stranger late at night in an empty train station, she has no idea what trouble it contains. She is on her way to a new life at the remote house of Plas-y Fran, but when she gets there the happy family Christmas she had hoped for turns out to be an illusion. Because Tomos has been missing for a year and a day, and if the strange and dangerous Family have really taken him, who would be mad enough to try and get him back?

Armed with a talking bird who might not be telling the truth, a magical snow-globe and her own indomitable courage, Seren sets off on a journey into a midnight world of snow and stars, to an ice palace unlocked only by a Door of Blood and Tears.

The Clockwork Crow is a gripping Christmas tale of enchantment and belonging, set in a frost-bound mansion in snowy mid-Wales, from a master storyteller.

Winner of the Tir na n-Og Award

**Shortlisted for the Blue Peter
Book Awards**

**Shortlisted for the Independent
Bookshop Week Book Award**

**Included in the BookTrust
Great Books Guide**

Nominated for the Carnegie Medal

The Velvet Fox

Book two in the award-winning
Clockwork Crow trilogy

(Firefly Press, 2019)

Orphan Seren Rhys is enjoying her first summer at Plas-y-Fran. But as autumn arrives, it brings with it a mysterious new governess who seems intent on separating her form her new home.

Dangerous figures from a bewitched toy carousel stalk the house and, fearing the worst, Seren calls on the clockwork crow to help her. But can he reach her in time, and will they be able to escape the magical creatures threatening to ensnare them, led by the Velvet Fox?

'Darkly menacing and creepily atmospheric.'
Sally Morris, *Daily Mail*

'Fisher writes with elegant poise. *The Velvet Fox* will charm and frighten readers in equal measures.'
Philip Womack, *Literary Review*

'A writer whose own strange magic is impossible to resist.'
Daniel Hahn

'Catherine Fisher has woven her magic once more, twisting fairy tales, folklore and fantasy into a spellbinding tale.'
Family Bookworms

'There is humour as well as excitement in this excellent story of a brave and resourceful heroine who surprises even her mentor, the Crow.'
Books for Keeps

Firefly

www.fireflypress.co.uk